Rosie's Rescue

Raisa Stone

DEAR COMPANION PUBLISHING

www.ukrainiansoulfood.ca

Library and Archives Canada Cataloguing-in-Publication

Stone, Raisa, author
    Rosie's rescue / by Raisa Stone.

ISBN 978-1-4996-4527-9 (pbk.)

    1. Horses--Juvenile fiction. 2. Animal rescue--Juvenile fiction. I. Title.

PS8637.T6585R68 2014   jC813'.6   C2014-903659-0

Cover painting: Florence E. Valter (in the Public Domain)

DEDICATION

For all the boys and girls who love and protect animals, and the adults who support them.~ *Raisa Stone, Author*

CHAPTER ONE

Rosie soared over the jump on her great stallion. When they landed, she reined him into a tight stop. He reared on glossy haunches, coiling like an immense ebony spring. His long front legs danced across the sun, and flame shot from his eyes and nostrils.

Though the crowd's cheers were loud, Rosie calmed him with a murmur. She slipped off her helmet and gloves, ran a hand through her red blonde bangs and shook her long braid free. The stallion bowed his head. His rippling mane, so black it was blue, cascaded to his knees. Despite the chilly spring air, both girl and horse were damp with exertion.

"Right on, Rosie!" said her best friend Micheline, leaning on the handlebars of her own bike. "That's the first time I've seen anyone take the ramp, then pop three wheelies in a row."

Rosie's daydream landed with a thud! as solid as the one her tires made hitting the pavement. She picked at a thread on her fawn riding breeches, the fabric shiny with use.

"High five, Michie," Rosie said after a moment, raising her left hand. The girls' hands met with a smack, then clasped in a secret handshake. The shake had evolved into an elaborate ritual over the years. It now involved eight separate moves, the last of which was a back handed pinkie link.

"You're jumping beautifully too, Michie," said Rosie. "You'll get the sequence by the end of the week."

Micheline sighed and said, "Get real. I can't hold on to even one wheelie. I'll never be able to do this trick." She ran her hand along the lone scratch on her bike's red top tube. The girls had insisted on buying boys' bikes after discovering the absent tube on girls' was to accommodate long skirts.

"I feel like I'm done for the day. Do you want one more try?" Rosie asked.

"No, I've had enough," Michie replied. "Let's go."

"Things will be better when we have real horses."

"I can hardly wait. We'll ride together every day."

"Every single day," Rosie echoed.

They walked their bikes down the street, giving them quieting pats as if they were cooling down show horses. Michie popped three pieces of gum in her mouth and blew a pink bubble ten inches across. She was the school bubble champ, renowned for never getting gum stuck in her hair.

They'd been inseparable in the six years since kindergarten. They'd one-upped each other collecting from the tooth fairy, teamed-up to bean a bully with their lunch bags, and up-dated the school library with a petition for better books.

After another high five and "Best friends forever!" the girls said goodnight.

At her back door, Rosie propped her bike on its kickstand. She pulled a white flannel cloth from her pocket and gave it a quick shine. "There you go, boy," she said, and patted the shining surface. The black lacquer was as pristine as when her parents helped her buy the bike.

Rosie spied a tiny, oddly shaped ball on the door mat. She scooped it up gently in her gloved hands. To her delight, small brown legs began to uncurl in her palm.

The door opened, and the kitchen's warmth reached towards her. "What you have there, poopchik?" asked her grandmother in a heavy Ukrainian accent.

Rosie showed her. "This little spider is almost frozen. I

wonder why she was outside when it's so cold?"

"Weather in British Columbia so crazy, sometime creature surface before warm enough," replied her baba.

"I'd like to keep her in my room," said Rosie, looking into Baba's face for a reaction. "I need to learn more about animal first aid. If I'm not getting a horse yet, I'll work with what I've got." She stuck out her lower lip. "I'm going to put her on a plant and see if she comes around."

And that's what Rosie did.

Then she sat cross legged on her bed and flipped through a book called *Pets in Trouble*. "Spider, spider, spider," she muttered. "Here's iguana, hamster, dog, cat. No spider." She pulled at a strand of hair. "Oh, try 'cold.'"

Baba poked her head in the open door. "How you doing?" she asked.

Rosie ran a finger down the Table of Contents. "Here it is!" she said. "What to do when an animal has a cold. Hmmm. Symptoms. Hey, spider, are you sneezing?" she called towards the plants. "Not that I noticed."

She jabbed at the page. "It says here I'm supposed to take her temperature. Not a chance. Where do you put the thermometer on a spider?"

"Hoo boy," said Baba, false teeth clacking. She sat on the bed. "Just think more deep about research topic."

She flipped back a few pages, where Rosie could see another reference to 'cold.'

Rosie smacked her forehead. "Duh. She doesn't *have* a cold. She *is* cold. The little spider has hypo-ther-mi-a." She sounded it out. "My brain is rattled from all the jumping I did today. Don't worry spidie, help is coming. Even if it's a little slow." She moved her bookshelf lamp close to the window and switched it on so it shone directly on the plants. "There, now you'll warm up."

"Good research job," said Baba.

"Yeah, with a little help," Rosie answered, grinning.

"That's okay," Baba replied. "Vet have assistant. I come for pay cheque Friday."

"Baba, what was that song you used to sing about spiders? It had something about good luck."

Rosie hummed a few bars.

"I sing you whole thing later, with Mom and Dad help, too. Very nice song."

That night, Rosie couldn't see the spider anywhere. She pushed aside the plant leaves, but had no luck. It was pointless to look among all the animal books and ornaments that lined the walls of her bedroom. *The Black Stallion* series alone took up most of the bookshelf near her window, cheek to cheek with *Self Help For Your Goat* and *Wombats I Have Known*. Rosie didn't have a horse, a wombat or a goat, but she could dream.

She said, "Goodnight, spider," anyway, and went to sleep.

The next morning, she woke to a beautiful web woven across the corner of her bedroom window. The threads looked as if they were made of the thinnest glass. The little brown spider was busily lowering herself to the neat row of plants on the window sill. She landed on a leaf, and waved a leg. Rosie waved back, then quickly lowered her hand. "That was weird," she said, and gave her head a shake. She pulled on a chenille housecoat, walked down the hall and knocked on Baba's door.

When they returned, the spider was sitting on a spoke of her gleaming web. She hovered over a tiny fly, her legs describing circles as if she were casting a spell. Baba squinted up at the spider. "She very nice, Rosie," she said. "Her markings pretty, very clear. She small, but have nice strong leg for hunting."

"She's good at hypnotizing flies, for sure. And I had a feeling she's a girl. But how can you be sure it's a female spider?" Rosie asked.

"Look very close, Rosie. See how she have two tiny leg in

front bugeye face?"

Rosie stood on tiptoe and squinted, then nodded "yes."

Baba continued, "Those legs skinny all way down to feet. Man spider have fat ankle and big feet."

"I think she's a Wolf spider," said Rosie. "They're called that because they're great hunters. I'm glad, because I love wolves."

"She also little bit too hairy to be normal. You love *all* animal, Rosie. You be very fine doctor veterinary when you older." Baba put her hand on Rosie's head and stroked the wavy hair. "Listen, I have idea for name. Was name of my spider in Old Country," she said.

"I'd like to hear it, but I want something original," Rosie replied. "I'm going to get ready for school now. See you at dinner."

Baba trundled off to her room, grumbling something about, "Modern original Canadian idea."

"I'm getting soft on a spider," Rosie muttered as she brushed her teeth. Toothpaste dribbled onto her denim shirt. "Aaaaaargh," she said.

After school, she invited Micheline over. They puddle jumped on the way. By the time they got to Rosie's, splashes of muddy water marked their jeans to the knees. "Come on, Michie, let's play *Monopoly*. This time I'm going to scoop Park Place *and* Boardwalk."

"I don't think so," Micheline replied, hands in the back pockets of her jeans. "I've learned to control dice with my mind." She rocked on the toes of her sneakers. Her dark hair swung from a ponytail, neatly held with a red elastic. She was lean compared to Rosie's roundness, and taller by four inches.

Rosie snorted. "I've got a killer game on. Show me the money, psychic."

The afternoon light in her bedroom glowed softly on the sky blue walls, and streaked across the buttery yellow rug.

The little spider was busy doing spider push-ups in the middle of the horse pattern quilt. Up down up down, rock from side to side. Up down up down, rock from side to side. The afternoon sun gleamed off her creamy markings. Micheline shrieked.

"Sssshhhhhh," Rosie put a finger to her lips. "You'll scare my new friend."

"Yaya-you ha-ave a sp-pi-der for a p-p-pet?" stammered Micheline. Her body was vibrating from head to toe. "Yuck! That's gross. You're a freakazoid. I always knew there was something wrong with you. You're weird. You're not like other girls, and everyone knows it!"

She ran out the door. Rosie shouted after her, "That was nasty, Michie!" When she turned around, the spider had disappeared.

She slumped into the living room, where Baba and her parents were drinking sweet black tea. "What that terrible commotion?" asked Baba. Her white, curly hair peeked out from under a flowered black *babushka*.

Rosie took a cookie from a plate. "Michie freaked out on my spider," she replied between bites, and repeated what Micheline had said. "She's a coward. I'm sick of always being the brave one. One little spider, and she called me all sorts of names. I don't want to hang out with her anymore."

"I see," said Baba. She glanced at Mom and Dad, who were staring intently at Rosie.

"I don't blame her for freaking out," said Mom. "By the way, look at your jeans. What have I told you about taking care of your clothes?"

"Rosie," said Baba, "Please go get basket of *pysanky* I make."

"What do Easter eggs have to do with spiders? Rosie asked indignantly. She flounced to the living room and brought back the woven basket to the table anyway.

The basket was heaped with vivid Ukrainian eggs. There

was a yellow egg with dark orange stags chasing endlessly in a circle, a sky blue one with golden sheaves of wheat, and several with intricate patterns of triangles, dots and stars in many colours.

Baba reached in the basket, and carefully picked one out. "See, Rosie? I make spider web around this one." The egg was a dark rich red, with the web design artfully embellished by scarlet poppies and a yellow sun. While that part of the design was created by the usual wax-relief method, Baba had also formed tiny green leaves and vines with a miniature paintbrush, painstakingly curling them through the web's spiral. Baba began to sing in a rich contralto:

Before there was a world, there was
Grandmother Spider
Weaving the stars together
She made a web where people could live
She fed everyone
She brings all good things.

There are three friends
Caught in her web
The shining sun
The bright moon
And the light rain
To make things grow.

Weaving the stars together
She brings all good things
She brings all good things.

Rosie's dad added bass to the third verse:

Baba Spider weaves the web of life
She gives us the beauty of her designs
So all people can be together

Be kind to spider
And she will bring you good luck.

Mom's clear voice joined in the chorus:

Weaving the stars together
She brings all good things
She brings all good things.

Rosie had often heard her family sing together, but this time it was as if an enormous brass gong rang out inside her, and something ancient and true sang back. She felt her cheeks flush, and tears rose in her eyes. "That's beautiful," she managed to whisper.

The family sat silently for a few moments.

"That song many thousand years old," Baba said. "And that reason web design on our Easter egg important. I also add tree of life and sun, force that maintain life. You need protect little spider with all your heart, Rosie. But you need figure out how fix good friendship with Micheline, too."

"Wow. This is getting strange," said Rosie, and stood up. "I think I'll go check on the spider."

"Rosie," said Mom, "Often the best way to get past someone's fear is to educate them. Maybe you can sing the song to mend things with Michie. Not that I think she's the best you can do for a friend."

Rosie rolled her eyes and clenched her hands. "Oh Mom, that's so *Kumbayah* hippie girl. I am *not* going to school and sing and sway with my friends in the middle of the cafeteria. I'll tell them the creation story, though. The lyrics are great."

"This is a temporary situation with the spider, anyway," Mom replied. "The song is just a song. A story is just a story. You rescued the spider, but it doesn't mean it gets to stay. And she'd better not venture out of your room in the meantime."

"What you talking about?" asked Baba. "This creation

story. Without spider, we not exist. She as real as you or me. So is Rosie friendship with Michie."

"Tem-por-ar-y situation," Mom repeated. "I don't think it's healthy for Rosie to be focused on a spider. Or on bike sports with another tomboy." Her eyes glittered behind her wire rim glasses. Her chestnut hair was set in a perfect flip.

"Let's just take this day by day," said Dad, glancing at each determined female in turn.

"This spider more important to Rosie than you know," said Baba.

"It can stay until the weather warms up," Mom replied. "Then out it goes."

"She," said Rosie. "The spider is a she."

She glared at Mom, then looked away and cleared her throat. "Well, I'm going to go see how the spider is doing. Michie gave her a shock. Screaming is *not* cool for an animal recovering from trau-ma." She flipped her nose in the air and stalked off to her room.

CHAPTER TWO

Rosie lay on the bedroom floor with her head propped in one hand. The little spider had apparently recovered from The Incident. She walked confidently around Rosie's bed, now and then stopping to raise a skinny leg in a loose question mark.

"You look like a dog when it's thinking. Or peeing on a post," Rosie said. "I guess you're figuring the place out, huh? Mom and Dad just sang me this song, where I learned some amazing things about you. I wonder what kind of good luck you'll bring us?" She raised herself to a sitting position and put her hands on her middle, between her heart and belly. "There's a strange feeling inside me, like I want to laugh and cry at the same time. It's kind of embarrassing."

The spider came closer, stopped for a moment at the vibration of Rosie's voice along the floor, then scuttled into the closet. "Oh, you're shy. But that's a good idea, girl," said Rosie. "Dad says we're all too busy to clean corners around here. You'll probably find a dead fly or two behind my running shoes, because I sure don't vacuum there."

Baba leaned against the door frame. "Is spider get over screaming meemie?" she asked. She was wearing her favorite cardigan, ribbed dark red wool with buttons down the front. It stretched so tightly across her sturdy body that only the two buttons on the chest were fastened.

"Yeah, I think so. I'm figuring out how to keep my friendship with Michie," Rosie replied, "Especially after what she said. She's mean."

"You will," said Baba. "She said mean thing, but you need be patient with your friend. She not so confident like you. Very small thing can set her off."

"Well, I think she could try harder," Rosie replied. "So could Mom."

"I talk to Mom little bit. About Michie, you have to understand something..."

"What? I know she's adopted, but that was a long time ago. What else do I need to understand?"

"Nothing. Dinner in twenty minute," Baba said after a moment.

Rosie changed into her oldest jeans and *Singers Rule* t-shirt. After a phone call to her friend Peggy, she set the table with flowered plates and large sturdy water glasses.

Peggy arrived carrying a book called *Myths R Us* and wearing one of her ethereal tunics, with swirling designs in pastel blues and greens. Her ash blonde hair hung to her shoulders, held by a white velvet band.

Rosie showed her the spider, and Peggy nodded. She listened quietly to Rosie's rendition of the Baba Spider song chorus. Peggy *often* listened quietly. She was like a deep, cool lake, flowing effortlessly around obstructions. Her presence was a small holiday in Rosie's world of fiery loudmouths.

They all sat down at the dinner table. Mom carried in a baked vegetable casserole, topped with bubbling cheese. Dad set down a large bowl of brown rice. Rosie helped herself. "Yuck. I hate mushrooms," she said.

"Rosie, we've talked about this," said Dad. "Just put them on the side of your plate. As long as you eat the rest of it."

The spider name discussion started over dinner. "How about *Black Beauty*?" asked Mom sarcastically. She picked at the bare spoonful of casserole on her plate.

"No way, Mom. Like you can name a spider after a horse.

That's lame!" Rosie replied.

"Then I suppose *Merrylegs* is out of the question," said Peggy, blinking. "You'd better hope the spider doesn't get big enough to ride, either. What would you feed her?"

"I don't even want to think about something like that. I have my limits," Rosie answered.

"My spider in Old Country named Hanya Oksanichka Sophia Slowka Alexandrichka," declared Baba. "She name after ancestor. She big as man's hand and live fifty year. Every day she eat pile of bug as high my ankle."

She lifted her long skirt to show the beige support hose puddled around her swollen ankles. "I had beautiful horse, white like snow with dark eye. When sun shine, she look like silver. She name Misha. One day Stalin soldiers come to make this collectivization. One try to steal my Misha. Spider drop, pow! on his head and bite him till he die."

She mimed a huge spider with two hands, and dropped them, bang! on the table. Everyone jumped in their chairs. Cutlery clattered to the floor. "Then," she looked each of them in the eye, "I feed him to spider."

Rosie startled. A piece of broccoli fell out of her mouth. Dad shook his head "No," but Baba ignored him.

"Don't be worry, Rosie," said Baba. "I only feed one piece at time, so she not be sick. I give rest to neighbour. He make good leftover. I'm hungry, too, but have big trouble digesting Communist." She patted her ample belly.

Dad waved his arms, "Stop!" A mushroom flew off his fork and landed in Mom's water glass. Peggy stopped eating entirely and just stared at Baba.

Baba continued. "Then very terrible thing happen. Next soldier, he too much for spider. She bite his head, but his hair very thick. He take my beautiful Misha away." Baba looked at the floor. "Next thing I know, Soviets steal *all* horse, cattle and even our land. Is terrible thing. Then they make me work on collective farm for peanut."

Rosie made a tiny noise in her throat and put her arm

around Baba's shoulder. Baba looked down for a moment. Peggy nodded her head understandingly. Dad had put his face in his hands, and was slowly shaking his head back and forth. "Mama, we left terrible times behind us in Ukraine. I wish you wouldn't scare children with old history," he said.

"It'll be okay," said Mom in a soothing voice.

Baba gave Dad a piercing glance, then addressed Rosie and Peggy. "You forget history, you invite to happen again. Rosie, you always, always pay attention to what politician doing, no matter what country. In Ukraine, things done to us with violence. Here, many thing done very quiet, very polite, men wear suit and carry briefcase. They smile in your face. They take away one your right here, one program there, and then boom! next thing, your whole world gone. Can happen anywhere. Don't be fool."

"Okay Baba," Rosie said, mesmerized. This information wasn't new to her. When the school board cut funding to the Art program, her family was the first to organize a protest and help raise money so classes could continue. But Baba was on a roll tonight.

Mom nodded vigorously at her words, saying, "Mmmm-hmmm, mmm-hmm. Rational action is everything." Peggy's eyes grew rounder and rounder.

Baba continued with her story. "Anyway, I have to leave spider behind with neighbour when we finally run from Ukraina to Canada. Very sad. But my spider, Hanya Oksanichka Sophia Slowka Alexandrichka, she write me letter for many year. More faithful than your brother," she looked solemnly at Rosie's Dad with large brown eyes. "We call spider 'Rosie', for shortness."

"Okay Mama, that's enough," Dad replied. "We did *not* name you after a spider, Rosie."

"Then why is my middle name Hanya?" she asked. Peggy looked quickly away, smiling.

Mom began to speak, but Baba interrupted, "Why you not call your spider like my spider?"

"I'm sorry for what happened to you, Baba, but I want a special name for her, " Rosie said, giving her another affectionate squeeze on her shoulder. "It can't be like any other."

"My, I'm full," said Mom, pushing her chair away and patting a belly substantially flatter than anyone else's at the table. "I'll bet I gained five pounds."

A few minutes later, Dad called from the living room. A jug of apple juice sat on the coffee table. Mom and Dad sat side by side on the big couch and opened encyclopedias while Rosie and Peggy flipped through the myths book and surfed the Internet. Baba flipped casually through a fashion magazine. Her forehead wrinkled over the elaborate ads, and she sucked on her teeth.

Rosie decided she'd like to combine the name of the Greek goddess, *Diana*, who hunts for food and protects people, with *divchyna*, the Ukrainian word for a young woman.

"*Divana* is a great original name," she said. "We could even call our punk band that."

"Excellent choice," said Dad. "The band, however," Dad continued, "We'll discuss later."

"Oh Dad," said Rosie, "All you have to do is clean out half the garage, and we can start rehearsing."

"I play wicked bass," said Peggy.

"As Rosie's dad said," Mom added, "Later."

Baba grunted. "Divana. Sound like some kind modern name these people make up who dancing with crystal on head and moaning in park," she said. "One day they Greek god, next day they some kind rootsy-tootsy Gypsy. Only can't sing."

Mom snorted.

"They should try keep up dancing, singing with me and other women at Ukrainian festival. They think they New Age. Ha!" Baba spat into the dirt of a large plant by the couch. "I show them old age. Divana-Shmivana."

Baba glanced at Rosie and her voice softened. "But you

like name Divana, we keep Divana. I get used to it."

"Yes, Baba, that's what I'd like to do,"said Rosie. She crossed her arms and lifted her chin.

"Your little spider really is a diva," said Peggy. "She acts like she owns your bedroom window. Did she sing to you last night?"

"That's so crazy!" Rosie replied, laughing.

"If she could sing, she'd sound like this." Peggy fervently clutched her chest and made a series of high-pitched fluting sounds. Her long, tapering fingers with perfectly oval fingernails made the clownish act graceful.

Rosie put her hands over her ears. "That sounds like that boooooring concert the school made us go to. The singer looked like her underwear was too tight." She sucked in her cheeks and raised her eyebrows as high as they'd go, then moved her lips like a goldfish's.

"She sounded like it, too," blurted Peggy, then blushed at her rudeness.

"Never mind. Now *we* sing!" said Baba. She led the Spider Song, in a voice rich with feeling. Rosie closed her eyes tight. She sensed a web spinning inside her. It stretched towards Baba, and beyond. She dissolved into the web of life that stretched over her family, weaving them inseparably with the fertile land from which they'd come.

When they sang, "She gives us the beauty of her designs/So all people can be together," Rosie could see a young woman in the Old Country, galloping her Misha bareback across the green fields, red gold braid flying like a flag. Just behind her, a mere shadow, was Rosie on a dark horse. A hot shiver ran up her spine, and her arms filled with goosebumps.

Baba repeated the song, and Rosie sang along until she knew all the words. "Come on, Peg," said Rosie.

"No thanks," Peggy replied. "You're the singer."

"I know exactly what I'm going to do about Michie," Rosie said in a determined voice.

"What you decide?" asked Baba.

"Tomorrow I'm going to sing the Baba Spider song at school. I don't feel the least bit dumb or shy about it now."

"No way," said Peggy. "Why would someone with a voice like yours feel shy?"

"Yeah, you guys are always telling me I have a good voice. If I sing, the rest of them will understand why I have a spider in my bedroom. They'll probably even end up thinking it's cool."

"It *is* cool," Peggy replied.

"I'm always telling you what a good voice you have, Rosie," said Mom.

"Yeah, but you're my *mom*, so it doesn't really count," Rosie replied.

Mom sighed.

"Sure it count! And that very good idea, Rosie," said Baba. "Was first thing mama say to you, earlier. Many time you can teach people with song or story what they not listen to otherwise. You practice now, you win *American Idol*, too. I be in front row, show that Jennifer Lopez thing or two. Ha Ha!" she whooped. She crossed her arms and kicked out her feet, resplendent in fuzzy blue slippers.

That night in bed, Rosie hugged her royal blue comforter and sang over and over to herself:

Weaving the stars together
She brings all good things
She brings all good things
She brings all good things.

The moon glowed lemon yellow through Divana's web. Rosie felt its powerful pull along the strands of the one she sensed deep inside. She moved the setting on the Protection Dial in her heart from *Not Completely Sure* to *Wide Open*. Something good was coming soon. She knew it.

CHAPTER THREE

The cafeteria smelled of French fries, overcooked broccoli and something unfoodlike Rosie couldn't identify. Near the end of lunch hour, she asked her friends to help section off a corner of the cafeteria with orange plastic chairs.

Tummy fluttering, she snuck into the band room and grabbed a microphone and stand. She'd worn faded Levi's and her lucky top. She'd won two events at the district bike rally in it, and it seemed like a good choice for winning back a friendship.

Rosie gave the stretchy blue t-shirt a tug, took a deep breath and sang into the mic, pretending it was plugged in. Peggy played along on her acoustic bass. The instrument was six inches wider and eight inches taller than Peggy, and she had to stretch her arms to reach the full length of the strings.

Rosie swayed to the melody of the spider song, her eyes tightly closed, indicating the web with broad gestures. As the song rose to its final chorus, she got louder and made weaving motions with her hands. Her strong voice resonated against the tiles and steel fixtures.

Micheline, Barb and Shelley listened with blank faces. Aleisha smiled so that her dimples showed. When the song was done, Peggy said, "We named Rosie's spider last night, too."

Micheline blew a small gray bubble, then popped it with a

loud snap. She looked back and forth from Rosie to Peggy, then stood up and took a step towards Rosie, arms lifting as if to hug her. Rosie lifted her own arms. Michie glanced at the other girls. Her face reddened and she halted. Looking down at her shoes, she said, "Well, uh, that was different."

Barb said, "Michie told us about your spider. I'm *totally* grossed out. I don't even want to hear you sing again, freak." She picked up her patent leather purse and left. "That goes for me too, *spider girl*," said Shelley, and followed her out.

Aleisha sat quietly, head tilted to one side. She frowned. Her zigzag cornrows caught the light, and for a moment, it seemed to Rosie the rows stretched to eternity.

"I guess I could still do bike stuff with you sometime, Rosie," Michie said, looking over her head after the departing girls. "I don't know if I'll go in your house, though."

"Sure, Michie," said Rosie. "Bike stuff."

Micheline picked up her red knapsack and walked quickly away.

Rosie's heart felt as if it were bleeding a gazillion glass splinter Valentines.

Brad, Mark and Stefan had listened from a nearby table. They each got up and went to Rosie. "That was awesome," said her Ukrainian friend Stefan. Mark nodded. Brad gave her a light punch in the arm. Her head swam, and she focused on his black t-shirt's red rock band logo. Focused hard.

"Rosie," said Brad. "Let it go. Just. Let. It. Go."

The one o'clock buzzer was piercing, but Rosie barely heard it through the roaring in her ears.

Aleisha stood up and put her hand on Rosie's shoulder. The bell sleeve of her dark yellow sweater slipped up her arm, revealing a thin gold bracelet set with lapis. She said, "My grandmother tells me African stories about the trickster spider god, Anansi. I'm sure she'd tell them to you, too. Now let's get to class, singer."

She gave Rosie a light push, and the group left the cafeteria. Stefan, Aleisha and Rosie quickly set up the microphone and stand in the band room just as the teacher was entering. Stefan gave him a dazzling smile and said, "We love your class so much, we practiced at lunch."

"That's great. But next time, ask permission."

"Sure thing," Rosie replied.

A few days later, Rosie and Baba made borshch together. A heap of shredded cabbage and chopped dill lay ready by the cutting board. The kitchen was richly fragrant with the smell of boiling oxtail, and onions and garlic frying in plenty of butter. Their fingers were stained reddish purple from peeling beets.

On a chair sat Baba's cloth shopping bags. One was stenciled with, *If mama ain't happy, ain't nobody happy.* The other had a bird silhouette and said *Ducks Unlimited.* Beside them was Rosie's new book, *Arachnids I Love Too Much.*

"Hand me that dish of white bean, Rosie," Baba said. "Don't you like cute way they turn pink in borshch?"

Rosie grunted, "I guess so." As she nibbled on a carrot she was supposed to be grating, she asked, "I was wondering why Divana knew to show up at our house when she was freezing? You know, lots of people kill spiders."

'That is good question," Baba replied, wiping her hands on her *Blues Mama* apron. "Creature can sense where people are kind. Or you think maybe it's because when I give you seedling, your first choice was spider plant?"

Rosie stared at Baba. She said, "That's the dumbest joke I ever heard," then began laughing. They laughed so hard, they nearly forgot to stir the soup.

One week later, the family had great good luck.

CHAPTER FOUR

Baba met Rosie at the door, waving her hands. "You won't believe what happen! That little farm we been driving by for several year, they make sale. Your dad call. Family have just enough money in the bank for deposit."

"It's true," said Mom.

Rosie covered her mouth with both hands and let out a muffled shriek of joy.

"They have barn, Rosie," Baba continued with a grin. "You will get beautiful horse now, and not have to pretend with crazy bike. There is nothing in world so good like owning land."

Rosie jumped up and down, her long braid bouncing. Baba leaned forward and pushed her false teeth right out, then snapped them back in.

"That's totally goofy. You haven't done that since I was little," said Rosie, and her laughter became nearly hysterical. Soon all three were laughing so hard they were holding on to each other, tears running down their faces.

"Divana brought us this good luck," said Rosie.

"That's pushing it way overboard," Mom replied, stepping back with a serious expression. "We make our own good luck."

"We visit new home Saturday," said Baba, wiping her eyes.

"Do they have horses?" Rosie asked.

"Your father say something about there being couple in pasture."

"Cool! I hope I can pet them on Saturday. I can hardly wait till I get my own."

Baba just smiled.

Saturday couldn't come fast enough. Friday night, Rosie sat in a chair by her bedroom window, watching Divana lower herself to a plant after some juicy green aphids. The little spider waved a leg before settling in to eat.

Rosie waved back. "Thank you, Divana," she said. "We're so happy about the farm. I'm finally getting a horse. Baba will have a bigger room, and Mom is really excited about planting a garden. Dad is already looking at the new tools he's going to buy. You really do bring good things."

She picked up a pencil and began to sketch the spider.

Saturday afternoon, the family piled into their old Buick and drove to look at their new home. Rosie was wearing new black rubber boots with red toes. At the mall, she'd turned up her nose at the array of boots in white, blue and pink. "Those are babyish. I want what vets wear," she sniffed. "Let's shop at the hardware store."

The sky was a clear blue and the June weather unusually warm for Vancouver. It took the family forty minutes to drive from their East End home to the farm.

"Owner is very old, and she want to go live with her children and grandchildren in Ontario," said Baba. "We move right after your school get out, Rosie."

"Maybe they have a spider that brings good luck, too. Look at us. We have Baba living with us, and now their family will be together, too."

"Having your baba live with you is very good luck," Mom replied. Baba's face crinkled.

"And it has nothing to do with spiders," Mom added.

They pulled up to the white two story house. The door and windows were trimmed in deep blue. It was set well back from the road on ten acres, fenced with white posts and heavy wire. Two red chickens, each slightly larger than a baseball, were scratching in the front yard.

"Look, bantam chickens!" exclaimed Mom. "I had some as pets when I was little, Peep and Beep. They were so smart, I taught them tricks. I wonder if the owner is taking them with her?"

The real estate agent called, "Hello," from the porch steps. The family got out of the car.

"Mrs. McIvor is at home. She wants to give you a history of the place. Follow me," said the agent briskly, and led them into the house.

Rosie twirled her hair and fiddled with the buttons on her shirt as Mom and Baba opened cupboards and closets. The lady of the house looked frail, but she energetically told stories about her ornaments and furniture. Mom and Baba cocked their heads and made appreciative noises. Rosie was so bored, she scratched her arm just to look at the white streaks her nails made on the surface of her skin.

"Sorry," Mom said to Mrs. McIvor with a tight smile "All my daughter cares about are bikes and horses, and of all things, spiders. Sometimes I wonder if she'll ever act feminine, like her friend Peggy."

"Rosie fine way she is. You need..." Baba began. Rosie walked out the door.

She sat on the back steps, head in hand. She could smell the sunshine warming the yard. She raked her foot in the dust, forming the outline of a web. It was awkward going with a rubber boot. One sideways swipe, and Rosie blurred half the thread pattern. She erased it completely and started drawing a horse head with mane flying, but that made her nauseous with anticipation. She sighed loudly and scratched her arm again. The little red chickens pecked at a line of ants scuttling along the mossy crack in a paving stone.

She found Dad in the spacious tool shed, running his hands over the surface of a table saw and smiling dreamily.

"I'm going *mental.* I want to see the barn!" Rosie stamped

her foot.

"We'll wait for Mom and Baba," he replied sternly. "I'd like us to see it together. There's a surprise."

"Mom and Baba are taking forever. They're busy pretending they care about some old stuff," Rosie said, pouting.

"Rosie," said Dad. "That 'old stuff' is Mrs. McIvor's entire long, interesting life. It's as important to her as your horse books and bike. Or Baba's eggs. I already had my visit with her a few days ago. Selling this place is the hardest thing she's ever done. We're helping her say goodbye, and we must be respectful."

"Sorry. I'm just impatient."

"Me too."

After forever, Mom and Baba emerged from the house with the real estate agent. Mrs. McIvor followed, shutting the back screen door carefully behind her. The chickens cocked their heads at the group, and followed them down the short path toward the barn.

The path was lined with colourful flowers, bushes and large shade trees. Rosie was quiet, but the rest of the group chatted excitedly, commenting on the surroundings. Mrs. McIvor answered Mom's and Dad's questions about caring for the garden. The chickens punctuated their sentences. "Peep!" said one. "Beep!" said the other.

The small barn was painted a cheerful red. The large garden plot was beside, handy to the manure compost and a water tap. A long green hose was curled around a bracket. The little chickens pecked at oat grains by the barn door.

"Just like a barn and garden are meant to be," Mom sighed. Then she asked casually, "By the way, will you be taking those bantams with you to Ontario?"

""Oh no dear," replied Mrs. McIvor in a soft Scottish accent, "Birds are quite delicate, you know. You can have them, if you like."

Mom ducked her head. "Yes. Thank you," she replied. She

didn't say anything else for a long time.

The barn door opened into a space rich with the wonderful smells of hay and horses. Bales of straw and hay were piled against the far wall. An open door on one side revealed a small room. Rosie could see saddles and bridles on racks and hooks. She closed her eyes and inhaled the fragrance of leather polished with plenty of saddle soap. Three large box stalls faced a barn aisle that was swept clean.

Baba craned her neck to take in the details of the barn. "This lovely place. You keep very clean. Is healthy for horse," she said. Mrs. McIvor dipped her head in acknowledgment.

A bright chestnut gelding poked his friendly head over a stall door. A green stem hanging limply from his mouth added to the comical effect of the wide, crooked blaze on his face. "This is Billie," said Mrs. McIvor. "He's a love. Wonderful old half-bred hunter. He'll do anything you ask of him. Won't you, boy?" She stroked his neck. Despite painfully gnarled knuckles, her hand on him was firm.

A nicker sounded, and a finely chiseled black face with a white star appeared at the door to Billie's right. "And this is dear Jessie. She's packed my grandchildren around at many a Pony Club meet. I brought them in from pasture to make it easier for you to meet them, Rosie."

"Is this the surprise, Dad?" Rosie asked, her eyes shining. She stroked each of the long faces in turn. "Their noses are like velvet."

Mrs. McIvor answered Rosie. "Your family has more of a surprise in mind than just you petting them, dear. Shall I?" Rosie's parents nodded.

"You see, I won't risk my dear friends on the long trip across the country. Your family is buying them along with my house. They're very well trained and safe for a beginning rider. But not so old they won't bring a great deal of pleasure to your family for years."

Rosie had been holding her breath, and now she gasped. "Is that true?"

"They belong to us in one month," said Baba. "But you need promise you clean stalls and feed them five day from seven. That mean you get up early and come home by five o'clock. You ready for this?"

"For sure. I'll do anything for my own horse," Rosie replied. "I want to ride Jessie first."

"Rosie, I think that Jessie be perfect size for you. Good personality, also," Baba observed.

"I think so too," said Mom. "Although it wouldn't hurt you to lose weight so you don't outgrow her."

Baba bared her false teeth and puffed, then turned to Dad, "That big red guy, he remind me of horse you love in Ukraina, name Bosco. Remember? I catch you in pasture, teach him to drink beer from bottle. Oy yoi yoi, I be mad. I make beer for your father and me to drink Saturday night, not for horse."

Dad cleared his throat. "Yes, I remember, Mama. Anyway, let's talk about Rosie."

Mrs. McIvor chuckled. "I'll put Rosie up on each of them for a short while today. But I'll have to lead them." She turned to Rosie's parents. "Your girl *has* to take lessons, you know. These two will take care of her, but it won't do to have my lovelies' soft mouths yanked about. Jessie, being Anglo-Arab, is especially sensitive."

Rosie turned a direct gaze on her family. "I really want lessons, and I want to join Pony Club, too."

"One more thing, Rosie," said Mrs. McIvor. "I rescued Jessie at the meat auction. She'd been neglected terribly as a baby. Her mama was so starved, she didn't make it. As a filly, Jessie was wild as a hare. It was ages before she'd approach me unless she was desperately hungry and I was carrying a milk bottle or some oats."

"The poor thing. Will she trust *me*?" asked Rosie.

"You're a gentle girl, so I think eventually she'll trust you completely. But there are times she's not quite sure of herself, and you'll have to give her some of your confidence.

She never gets mean, but she might occasionally be aloof," she replied, tracing the star on the black forehead. The mare nudged her and snorted.

"Oi yoi yoi." Baba clucked sympathetically and shook her head back and forth. "World full these situation, for both animal and people." Her voice become upbeat. "We already call riding teacher you recommend," she said. "Rosie been on friend horse many times. She sit very good on horse. But she have first official lesson tomorrow."

Rosie's round face glowed with happiness.

She rubbed her face against Jessie's flat cheek, inhaling the delicious horse scent. Her red blonde hair made a sharp contrast to the ebony coat. "When I'm good enough, Jessie, I'll ride you everywhere," she said quietly.

She felt a tug up near her heart. Something slow and golden revolved strongly inside her. The web was strengthening, weaving her into her future. She felt a tingling sensation spread through her belly as she breathed into Jessie's tender nostrils, as every horsewoman in history has done since the beginning of that great love affair.

"Is horse belong here, still outside?" Baba asked softly. She had walked over to the empty box stall on Billy's left, and was peering intently inside. The floor was thickly bedded with clean straw. The manger held a scoop of bright oats, and the water in the black rubber bucket was crystal clear. There was a strange expression on Baba's face.

"No," answered Mrs. McIvor. "That stall's been empty a long time. My husband kept his horse there, and I've been a widow for a great many years." She gently touched the stall door. Her gracefully lined face flushed. "I like to keep it up, in their memory."

Baba's eyes filled with tears. "I am widow too. And that stall will have beautiful horse again."

"A white one named Misha, right Mama?" said Dad, taking her trembling hand.

"Look!" Rosie said, pointing upwards.

In the far corner of the black mare's stall was a huge spider web, shining in the light that came in through the windows set high on the barn walls.

"Oh yes," responded Mrs. McIvor. "My goodness, I've had a spider in this barn for fifty years. There she is."

The family could see a large black shape moving slowly at the centre of the web. The woman continued, "Her name is Anna Sandra Sofia Shirley Alexandra, after my Scottish ancestors. She's a lucky spider. Do you know, she once dropped onto the head of a horse thief and bit the daylights out of him, right in this barn."

She turned and winked discreetly at Dad. The two of them had chatted about more than real estate on his previous visit.

Baba's mouth was hanging open. Mom and Dad looked at the ground, at the ceiling, everywhere but at Baba. The black spider inched towards the outside edge of her thick web, spinning more threads as she went.

Mrs. McIvor continued, "The thief was still rolling on the ground screaming when the police came to take him away. Not before I'd managed to give him a swift kick or two myself, mind you, " she chuckled. "He passed away in hospital. 'Death by misadventure', they called it."

Baba gave a hoarse, "Huh."

"My goodness, that little gem is worth her weight in gold," said Mrs. McIvor. "She eats half a pound of horseflies a day. I'm so sorry, though the horses are staying, I'll be boxing up the spider and taking her with me to Ontario. Fifty years is fifty years, you know."

"That's okay," said Rosie, smiling pleasantly. "We have our own lucky spider."

"Peep!" and "Beep!" said the chickens by the door.

CHAPTER FIVE

Rosie felt as if she was floating. A choking sensation gripped her. "Can we afford this farm *and* the horses?" she whispered.

Mrs. McIvor's ears were sharp. She gestured to Rosie's parents. "I'd like to speak with you outside for a moment," she said.

The real estate agent froze by the barn door. When she'd put her brief case on the cement step, it came unlatched. The two little red chickens had torn apart the papers inside and built a nest.

Mrs. McIvor glanced at the scene. "Yes, dear, they will do that," she called to the agent.

Rosie gently lifted the bantams out, snuggling their warm feathery shapes to her chest. "Oh you bad things," she crooned. "I hope you didn't eat paper with ink on it. I'd have to take you to the hospital in a chicken ambulance to pump your stomachs."

The agent mumbled something about, "Going back to corporate real estate," then quickly told Rosie, "It's fine, it's fine."

Mrs. McIvor turned back to Rosie's parents. Her face was filled with light as she said, "It means the world to me that this farm go to people who genuinely love it and will care for it. You have no idea how important it is that you happily agreed to look after Jessie and Billie, even when they get too old to ride. It's been their home since they were babies, and I want them to be here till the day they die. They can never go to an auction, where you just can't know what will happen to them."

"For sure they be with us," said Baba softly. "Is how horse should be treated. I never had chance in Old Country, but I do this for Jessie and Billie. And no need police. I take care of any horse thief myself!"

"I'm sure you will," Mrs. McIvor replied. "I couldn't hope for a family better suited for my farm. Why don't we go in the house and discuss a fair price?"

The agent straightened up and put her hand to her forehead as if she was getting a really bad headache. She whispered, "Corporate real estate. Big commissions," one more time. The chickens in Rosie's arms cocked their heads at her and peeped softly.

When the family came out of the house, Baba and Mrs. McIvor had their arms linked. "You make sure you get that white horse," Mrs. M whispered in Baba's ear.

Rosie's parents had settled on a price for the little farm they could afford, and the old lady was thrilled, too. Rosie reached out to hug Mom, who put her arms around her, then pulled away as soon as her fingers sunk into the soft flesh of her daughter's back. The withdrawal felt as sharp as if one of Rosie's internal organs had been punctured.

That evening, Rosie sat by the phone. She picked up the receiver, then put it down. Picked it up, dialed three numbers, sighed, then put it down. She twiddled a hay stem she'd shoved into her pocket at the farm.

Baba put down her shopping bags. "You going to phone Michie?" she asked.

"No. She'll get all weird about the spider in the barn," Rosie replied. "But I don't know who else would be excited for me about the horses."

"Rosie, you and Micheline been friend since babies. You can be excite about farm without saying word 'spider'."

"Fine," Rosie said. "I guess I need to learn how to not

always speak my mind. But how come you can?"

Baba put her hands on her hips. "What you mean? I am most polite person I know."

Rosie rolled her eyes. "Anyway, you're right. I'd feel pretty bad if we moved away and I didn't talk to her. But I think Aleisha and Peggy might actually become better girlfriends. They're more 'feminine', anyway. At least Mom will be happy."

Baba said, "It fine to be mad at someone for little while. But not okay to turn up nose at people, just because they show weakness. I have friend I go shop with, and friend I go to singles club with. First one good at bargains, but not much fun. Other one like to laugh, but not have much hay in loft." Baba pointed to her head. "Rosie, your mother love you. But don't allow her dictate what you know deep inside for yourself," she added.

"Alright, alright, I get it," Rosie said. "I've never heard Aleisha and Peggy even *mention* horses. I'll call Michie right now, and just tell her about the horses and chickens."

"You invite her to farm this summer, too," Baba replied. "You two so crazy about each other for six year, I don't know what you thinking to leave her out. I watch you hold hand to walk into kindergarten. She friend deep in your heart."

"Yeah, we've been friends a long time. I'm thinking about how she helped me learn to swim when I was scared. She held my hand in the deep end, too."

Tears welled in Rosie's eyes. One overflowed and meandered down her right cheek.

Baba brushed it away with a wrinkled brown hand. "That's what I'm talking about!" she said. "Don't be hard heart. This terrible way to live. Is only one step from hard heart to being abusing kind of person."

Rosie hung her head. "You mean like whoever hurt Jessie."

"Exactly," said Baba, nodding so vigorously the tail of her babushka flapped. "Tell me something. You turn your back on Jessie if she get scared one day? What if this make her bite you?"

Rosie was shocked. "Never," she said in the faintest whisper. She raised her voice. "Never, ever. An animal can't help if it gets scared. If Jessie bit me, I'd forgive her."

"Can you imagine how freak out Michie be, to say such mean thing and stop playing with you because of little spider?" Baba asked. "And now she so terrify to lose *any* friend she don't know what to do. Be patient with her. You very strong person, sometime you forget other people not like you."

Rosie hung her head.

Baba rummaged in her *Mama* bag. She handed Rosie a striped peppermint humbug and popped one in her own mouth. They sucked on the candy silently for a moment.

"We think of way to help her stop being scared of Divana," said Baba. "But you know, Rosie, she will never be so complete confident like you."

"Why the heck not?" asked Rosie.

Baba hesitated, then said, "That's just way she is."

"Well, I can swim enough to get by, but I'll never be a lifeguard. Michie has her bronze star already," said Rosie. "She's brave where I'm not. Besides," she added, "I love her."

"This most important thing," said Baba. "Don't you forget."

Rosie sniffled twice, picked up the phone and dialed.

CHAPTER SIX

Rosie was carefully wrapping her animal ornaments in tissue paper when Divana lowered herself on a thread, first to a plant, then hop! all the way to the floor. She walked around the dark wooden lamp table. Thump thump! Actually, with eight legs, it sounded more like thumpityTHUMP! ThumpityTHUMP! ThumpityTHUMP! Thump THUMP!

"Wow, Divana, that's loud. You're some heavy spider," Rosie said.

Rosie didn't have any more time to think about Divana's size that day. After a late Sunday lunch, she impatiently helped clear the dishes, then ran to her room to change into her new breeches for her first riding lesson.

She emerged from her room in snug charcoal-coloured breeches with the tag hanging out the back. Mom said, "Hmmm. They're a bit tight. Have you gained weight?" Rosie's face fell. Dad said nothing. "Anyway," Mom continued, "We have surprise for you. I'm going to put my hands over your eyes and walk you into the living room."

"Come on, I'm too old for that," Rosie answered. "You're always trying to keep me a baby."

"Oh fine, be rude girl," said Baba. She turned to Mom. "Here, you put hands over *my* eye, and you and me have all the fun."

Together, Mom and Baba swayed into the living room, giggling. They bumped into a dividing wall when their legs got tangled in Baba's long skirt, but they made it.

Rosie followed, then looked quickly around. "What's the big deal? I don't see anything different," she said.

"How about on door mat?" asked Baba.

"Oh!" Rosie's left hand flew to her chest. Gleaming softly on the mat was a pair of black leather riding boots. Faint hairline creases marked the ankles.

"That's why your dad was late for dinner other night," said Baba. "He find these on horse Internet. They get too small for girl. She wear them only in horse show. She win many time. They in great shape, very fine leather." She picked up one boot and stroked it before handing it to Rosie.

Rosie threw her arms around Baba's soft warmth. "They're beautiful, thank you!"

"They're made a bit wider in the calf, for your strong Ukrainian legs, Rosie," said Dad. After some tugging, Rosie got the boots on. They fit perfectly.

Off the family went. They drove up a long, winding lane shaded by Arbutus trees with peeling brick and gold-coloured bark. Horses of all shapes and sizes grazed in the fields on either side of the board fence. "I see two Paint ponies, a buckskin Quarter Horse, and a bay Thoroughbred," said Rosie.

The barn was weathered gray wood, and obviously hadn't been painted in years. A wheelbarrow stood by the manure pile, instead of the usual shiny tractor.

"Maybe coach not have much money either," said Baba. "But that Scottish woman recommend her. She say she been injured in accident and can't ride in horse show anymore. But she love teaching children."

"I looked her up on the Internet," Rosie said. "She was really, really good. She was even going to be on the Olympic team. Then she took a bad fall over a jump."

"See?" said Baba. "Not have to be fancy-shmancy to be

good. We same way. Barn is solid and horse well fed. That's all thing that matter."

"Yeah," said Rosie.

When the family entered the barn, Baba commented on how well-kept it looked. The coach met them dressed in clean jeans and short, shining paddock boots. Her streaked brown hair was tied back neatly in a bun. She came towards the family with her hand out, a small limp in her otherwise confident step.

She led Rosie's mount from a box stall and tied him to a large metal ring in the aisle. "This is Smokey," she introduced the tall, robust pony. He was gray, with rose-tinged dapples that connected from his rounded crest all the way to his even rounder rump. His face was white, with ears, eyes and lips outlined thickly in black.

"Crazy horse," said Baba. "He wear mascara."

"And eyeliner. He's beeeyoooootiful!" Rosie replied. She stroked Smokey's neck, and he pushed his face into her chest. "Look, he's a hugger," she said, cradling his rubbery whiskered chin in her
hand. He waggled it and sighed.

"He's very loving," said the coach. "He even plays uncle to the foals." She turned to Rosie's parents. "He'll take good care of her once she's on his back, too."

The coach showed Rosie a container full of interesting objects. Curry and mane combs, dandy and body brushes, a metal hoof pick and a soft cloth. "You'll use each of these tools on Smokey before and after you ride. It's his own set."

"Wow," said Mom. "They don't use half as much stuff on my hair at the beauty salon."

"They don't put a saddle on you either," said Dad. "Be grateful."

"You two very have strange sense humour," said Baba. "I don't know how Rosie so normal."

Rosie learned to use the brushes in turn. Smokey stretched out his neck and leaned into the pressure. Rosie nearly swooned from the wonderful smell of his coat. The coach showed her how to pick out his feet, telling Smokey, "Up", and then "Thank you," when he lifted a hoof. "Speak to him the whole time, Rosie," she said. "Whether you're riding or grooming, it's a constant communication."

Rosie whispered, "I talk to my pet spider."

The coach blinked, then replied calmly. "Well, it's unusual for someone to tell me about her pet spider, but talking to animals is perfectly normal. Does she talk back?"

"Yes. She waves her legs in different combinations. I understand her perfectly."

"Rosie, look at how Smokey is swiveling his ears and happily swishing his tail. You can tell what a horse is saying to you by his body language, too. Animals speak to us all the time. Your spider is probably telling you things quite specifically."

Rosie grinned. She definitely had the right teacher.

The coach had her finish by wiping the soft white cloth around Smokey's eyes and nostrils. "Now for a little polish," she said, "Run the cloth firmly over his entire body, head to tail, left side to right. Smokey will look like he's just been waxed at the car wash!"

Baba murmured, "She little bit strange, too. Car wash for horse. Only in Canada. I hope Rosie not get wild idea here."

"I don't think this is where she gets her wild ideas," said Mom.

When Rosie was done, Smokey gleamed like a silver trophy. Each hair of his mane was defined in the afternoon light streaming in through the barn windows. "At our friends' farm, we lead them in from pasture and just sort of quickly take off the dirt with an old brush," Rosie said. She kissed Smokey's soft sooty nose.

The coach helped Rosie saddle the pony, then clipped a long rope to his bridle. "Rosie," she said in a firm voice, "I'm going to control your horse with this lunge line. Today you will work on balance, and will not touch the reins." She fitted a faded black velvet hunt cap on Rosie's head. Rosie's fingers shook as she buckled up; it took her three tries.

"She strict teacher," said Baba. "Is good for Rosie. She really learn to ride horse!"

"I think she takes after you that way, mama," Dad said. "She's a natural horsewoman."

The group walked out to the ring, and the lesson began. Mom, Dad and Baba leaned against the fence.

"Walk on," said the coach. Rosie squeezed Smokey with her calves, and he stepped forward. The coach stood at the centre of the ring as if it was the hub of a huge web, with Smokey moving along an invisible strand. Rosie let her seat bones sink into the saddle. Watching the pony's ears flick back and forth sent a tingle through her middle.

The coach gave instructions for trotting. "Rising the trot is easier than sitting, and gentler on Smokey's back. It's called 'posting.' Now, head up and heels down!"

Round and round they went, Rosie rising and falling in the saddle. "Up down, up down, up down," chanted the coach. "That's it. You're riding to the left, so let his back push you up when his right shoulder comes forward, sit when his left does. 'Rise and fall with the shoulder to the wall.' Up down, up down."

"My spider posts when she's happy," said Rosie, a little breathless.

"I see," said the coach.

After half an hour, the coach unhooked the lunge line and patted Rosie's leg. "You've obviously been on a horse before. Next week I'll let you pick up Smokey's reins. If you do well, we'll have a canter."

Rosie dismounted. Her face was flushed and her legs shaky. The coach handed her the reins, then said to the family. "After Rosie has another lesson, she may join one of my groups," she said.

"You don't think Rosie's weight will hold her back, do you?" asked Mom.

Rosie felt like her mother had reached into her middle, pulled a plug, and drained the pleasure from her body.

The coach waited a beat. She said matter-of-factly, "You have a nice healthy girl here. She's athletic, and I can't see any difficulties. I was pressured to lose weight for my sport, and ended up very ill with an eating disorder. I made myself throw up my food, and I became too weak to ride. My 'accident' story in the press isn't the whole truth."

She turned back to Rosie and winked. "Good job. Now walk Smokey till his chest and flank feel cool." She walked towards the barn.

"Well, she sure told *us*," said Mom. A vein throbbed in her forehead, and she anxiously touched the sharp jut of her hipbones.

Baba followed as Rosie walked Smokey along the fence. "Better than good job," she said. "Soon you ride like Cossack. I put on *my* riding pant and show you hang upside down from saddle, pick up handkerchief from ground with teeth."

"Way cool, Baba," Rosie answered, stroking Smokey's neck. "I want to learn to do that, for sure. Can you show me how to stand up on his back while he's galloping, too? I bet none of the kids at my new school can do that."

"Sure thing, Rosie!" said Baba. "Cossack way is stand on *two* horse back, but we start easy first few week. After you learn that, you do target practice with bow and arrow from horseback. Then you be divchyna and goddess Diana, too. Kapow!" Baba squatted as if she was on horseback. Her long paisley skirt rode up to her swollen knees as she mimed shooting an arrow from a bow. "Very handy, we ever have to fight Russian again."

"It'll be a little while before she's ready for that, Mama," called Dad. He lowered his voice. "It'll be a while before any of us are."

"Sweet, Baba," said Rosie. "In the meantime I'll practice with Michie on our bikes. It won't be long before we're riding horses together, just like we planned."

Then she remembered. Even though they talked at school, Micheline hadn't met her for bike acrobatics since The Spider Incident. She'd sounded vague in yesterday's phone conversation. Rosie had found herself pushing at Michie's noncommittal responses with sarcasm. "I guess a little spider scared you right out of having fun with me, huh?" she asked, then dug her nails into her thigh.

Once, Rosie walked in on Micheline, Barb and Shelley in the bathroom. They were instantly silent, and Michie had avoided Rosie's eyes since. In the excitement of the new farm and horses, Rosie hadn't let it all sink in. Her nostrils filled with a faint scent of bubble gum and a wave of sadness shook her.

She and Smokey neared the corner where Mom and Dad were conferring.

"I think Rosie's taking after mama," Dad said.

Mom looked thoughtful. She gazed into Dad's eyes. "Good!" she said. "What more can you wish for your daughter? She'll fight for what she wants, and find happiness in the hardest circumstances, all her life. But she is *still* not going to keep that spider. It wouldn't hurt her to lose weight, either. I don't care what the coach says. Rosie is not realistic in so many ways."

Dad put his arm around Mom and squeezed. "Leave it alone, babe," he said gently.

Rosie walked past looking straight ahead. She laced the lock of mane on Smokey's sturdy withers through her fingers. Her knees felt shakier than when she'd dismounted.

Two days later, Rosie was putting on her runners when Divana fell out the right leg of her breeches and *whomp!* tumbled to the floor. She lay dazed for a moment, then scurried into the closet. Three days after that, she fell out the left leg and turned a somersault, whompity bump!

Rosie had refused to take off the breeks or wash the horse smell off her hands since her lesson. She only wore the tall black boots around the yard. She didn't want to risk scratching them on her bike.

"She ride in your clothes because you make feel warm and safe," said Baba. "She also think she horsewoman."

I wonder why she sounds so loud?" Rosie asked. "She seems to be gaining weight like crazy."

"Lots of juicy bug. She good, healthy Ukrainian spider with big bone and appetite," said Baba, "Just like us."

"Big bones? Do you think I'm fat, too? The girls at school always talking about 'diet this and diet that.'" Her forehead wrinkled. "Most of the time I think they sound really dumb, but sometimes I wonder if I should diet, too." She pinched the roll of skin at her waist. "Mom is so slim. Maybe she's right about me. I might get too fat to ride horses."

"No diet for you, Rosie," Baba replied. "Mom have some big problem with this. Food is one of great gifts that Baba Spider gave us. You what people in this country call 'chubby,' and you fine way you are. We pay good attention to nutrition, and that's all that necessary. Remember coach say how you athletic?"

"Yes. Will I be round like you when I'm older?" Rosie asked.

"If you lucky," said Baba. "Handsome men from Europe follow me down street, saying, 'Oooh baby.'"

Rosie scrunched up her face. "I'm not sure I want that to happen," I said.

Dad chimed in. "Ample bodies run in the family," he said, patting his own rounded belly. "That's how we survived for thousands of years when food was scarce."

"Being round is fine with me," Rosie said. "You're beautiful, Baba. But I got a bit worried when we were trying on t-shirts at the mall, and a couple wouldn't even fit over my head."

"Big brain, sweetheart, big brain," said Baba. "Clothes supposed to fit your body. It crazy thing to mess your body to fit clothes."

Dad cleared his throat. "Rosie, your Mom is struggling

with an eating disorder called bulimarexia, just like your coach."

"Well, duh. Mom runs to barf after every meal," said Rosie. "A girl at school told me what that's called."

Dad and Baba looked at each other. "She's started counselling, Rosie," said Dad.

"If she's in counselling, why is she being so mean?" asked Rosie. "She's always said things, but she's gotten worse."

"Most time when people first start facing truth about self, they very sad and angry. Is not about you, sweetheart," said Baba.

"Oh. Okay. I just wish I fit into skinny clothes," said Rosie.

"Someone else designed them from a vague idea about how yours is supposed to look," added Dad. "You know the strangest thing? It's mostly men who design clothes for females. But one size does not fit all."

"Oh," said Rosie. "That's pretty clever, Dad."

"I have my moments," he replied.

CHAPTER SEVEN

The next time Divana began her thumpity THUMP! Thumpity THUMP! Thumpity THUMP! Thump THUMP! on the wood floor the bedroom, Rosie lay down on her side, cheek against the blue throw rug by the bed. She was still wearing her riding breeches. They were stretchy and awfully comfortable for all sorts of activities, particularly lying on the floor. Her second best friend Stefan carefully removed the calculator and miniature slide rule from his belt and joined her. The pair watched Divana stride determinedly towards a dead fly in the closet. Thump THUMP! "You've gotten hungrier, Divana," Rosie remarked. "Oh man, what's that *thing* on her stomach?

"I don't know," said Stefan. "But it sure looks interesting."

"*Interesting?*" she said sharply, rising on one elbow.

"I meant that in a 'needs to be further explored because it may be cause for concern' kind of way," he hastily replied.

They searched through Rosie's animal books, but couldn't find a reference to an abdominal growth on a spider. The closest thing was a photo of a large, misshapen tumour on a dog's flank, labelled *Sarcoma*. Stefan sucked his breath between his teeth and reluctantly showed the page to Rosie. "Aaaaaaaaaaah," went Rosie, and pushed the book away.

She ran into the living room, where Baba was playing blues on the piano. "Yeah, I one honky tonk mama, just blue as I can be. That what I say. Ha!" she wailed while pounding the keys.

"Come quick!" Rosie cried, "Divana has cancer. She has

this huge freaky growth!"

"Calm down, sweetheart. Let's take close look," said Baba, walking towards Rosie's room. Mom trailed behind.

Divana had moved the first fly to a shadowy area of the closet, and was trying her fierce wolf spider hunting stance with a second. She raised herself as high as she could, up up UP on her skinny legs. But those legs were quivering slightly, and her large belly didn't quite manage to clear the floor. She tried again. Up up UP on her long legs. Then down a touch. She rocked a little on her belly.

"Look," said Rosie. "There's a big white ball on her stomach. She must be really far gone."

Baba slowly sank down on her arthritic knees and pressed her cheek to the dusty floor. "Hmmmm," she said, and coughed. Rosie lay on her side too, forehead wrinkling. Stefan made a trio. Mom stood behind them with crossed arms.

Baba burst out laughing. Rosie turned red and said through clenched teeth, "I don't think this is a good time to laugh."

Baba replied, "Everything fine with spider. That white ball full of baby Divana. No wonder she eating so much. She making herself strong to carry baby on her back when they born."

"Not cancer?" Rosie asked.

"Not cancer," said Baba. "No way."

Stefan said, "I read that a wolf spider has about a hundred babies."

"Hundred?" said Baba. "Ha! This Divana of yours Rosie, she so healthy, she probably make three hundred."

"Cool!" said Rosie.

"Three. Hundred. Spiders. In. The. House." Mom said. "That's *my* 'no way.'"

Baba went on. "My spider in Old Country, she make one thousand. Oi yoi yoi, air and food not so good here in Canada. Spider have less baby. Don't worry. You will have enough baby spider to bless friend and whole neighbourhood, too. Start taking order."

She mimed a waitress writing on a pad, then chuckled with glee. "Come on, we need start thinking name for baby."

Baba sat at the dining room table, hands folded in front of her. Rosie fetched an unused exercise book. Stefan rolled up the sleeves of his white cotton shirt and looked serious. He offered Rosie a ballpoint pen from the row in his front pocket, but she waved a package of fruit-scented markers at him. She picked out blue and red and wrote on the front, *Baby Spiders,* then quickly sketched Divana hanging from a thread. Mom looked on from the kitchen doorway, her face pale and tight.

"Ah ha!" said Baba. "Now you be happy we have good ancestor names for spider."

"Yes, Baba," Rosie replied. "I am. We have to have Hanya, Oksana, Sofia, Slowka and Alexandrichka. Those will be first one we see." Baba grinned, and Rosie wrote them down.

"And also Anna, Sandra, Shirley, Sophie and Alexandra, like the Scottish woman's spider," Rosie added.

Baba rolled her eyes. "Oi, these English names, they just not historical romantic. But okay. Now get serious. We got lots spider to name." She sniffed skeptically at a root beer-scented marker, pulling it back and forth from her nose and squinting at the printing on its side.

Just as Stefan suggested, "Chevy, Ford and Chrysler," Dad walked in the door, wiping dust from his jeans.

Rosie excitedly told him the news as he unbuckled his tool belt. He groaned and put a hand to his forehead. "Divana's having hundreds of babies? Does this mean I have to go out at midnight to buy her ice cream and pickles? That's what your Mom wanted while we were waiting for you, Rosie."

"Gross," said Rosie.

"I don't appreciate the comparison, *darling*," said Mom. The muscle on the side of her jaw flexed.

Baba glared at Dad. "No ice cream. No pickle. I fix special

spider *kutya*. Little bit organic wheat and poppy seed, lots crushed bug. My Hanya Oksanichka Sophia Slowka Alexandrichka eat whole bowlful at time. Divana very healthy for Canadian spider," Baba humphed, "But she eat only little bit on spoon. Then we say special blessing for healthy mother, healthy baby."

"Sounds like something *my* baba would do," said Stefan, grinning at Rosie.

"Your baba would feed spider big plate *perohi* with sour cream and onion, then teach her play bingo," Baba replied.

"Yeah? And who got my baba hooked on bingo?" asked Stefan playfully.

"You smarty pants boy," said Baba, wagging a finger.

"The kutya will be wonderful," Mom interrupted. She played with the gold chain on her neck. "But Rosie, we can't keep three hundred spiders in the house. Not even one hundred. In fact," she added through clenched teeth, "It's time to get rid of the one you already have. Before she spawns all over my house. This is ridiculous."

Rosie threw Mom a look. "You sang the Spider Song. Now we'll have three hundred times the good luck." She began sketching plant leaves on the cover of the exercise book.

"Look, the spider creation myth is a beautiful thing. I just think you're going too far."

"Either you look after animals, or you don't!"

"Can't you just drop them at the *Humane Society*?" asked Stefan.

"That shameful thing to say!" snapped Baba. "Spider is sacred animal!"

Stefan put his hands, palms forward, in front of his face. "Okay, okay. I was only joking."

Rosie was puzzled. "We give donations to the Humane Society," she said.

"To help animal whose owner don't take responsibility, Rosie," said Baba, her eyes snapping. "Animal powerless, and some people don't even know they have feeling, and they even talk to us.”

Rosie's eyes narrowed. “Then they shouldn't have them in the first place,” she declared. “Like when the neighbours left their dog chained in the yard all the time, with no shade or water.”

“Good thing you call Humane Society, then,” said Baba.

“That was you?” said Dad. “I wondered, when I saw their truck. You beat me to it!”

Rosie just smiled.

“Oh for goodness *sakes*,”said Mom. Her head trembled. “Spiders are wild animals, they can take care of themselves. The creation myth is important to us culturally, but it doesn't mean we have to take in all the world's spiders.”

“Surely there's a compromise possible here,” said Dad, spreading his hands.

“I don't think so,” Mom replied heatedly. “It's a *story*, not real life. Be reasonable, Rosie. The baby spiders will be fine outside. They'll be old enough to dig burrows in the ground before it gets cold.”

“You know, Rosie,” said Stefan. “Baba Spider created the world. She's been here much longer than humans, and she'll still be spinning the web of life when we're gone. Chill out.”

“Hey, whose side are you on?” Rosie asked. “Yeah, that's what she does in the *story*. But Divana's *my* real life responsibility. I took her in when she was frozen, and now she's pregnant. Baba Spider must have a reason for sending her to us, and I'm going to find out what it is. We're going to have hundreds of spiders around, and I need to protect them. No compromises, Dad.”

Dad rubbed the inside corners of his eyes and looked sideways at Mom. Her arms were crossed and her chin was lowered to her chest. “You're going to be living out in the garden with the spiders, Mr. Compromise,” she said.

“More than hundreds,” Stefan replied. “Do the math, Rosie. It won't be long before Divana is grandmother to thousands.”

"You do the math," said Rosie. "That's your thing. How many thousands?"

Stefan pulled the elaborate calculator from his belt. Even though he rarely ventured out of the neighbourhood, his device even had a GPS. "Let's see," he said, punching buttons with a flourish, "If Divana has a hundred babies and half of them are female..."

Rosie picked up his train of thought. "That's fifty spiders having a hundred babies each, next spring. No, wait. Fifty *one*," she amended. "You forgot that Divana will have more babies."

"Rosie, you're too smart for us," said Dad.

"That's what I been trying to tell you," mumbled Baba. "Is miracle."

"Okay," Stefan continued, "Fifty one spiders having one hundred babies each...."

"Means fifty one hundred baby spiders next spring!" shouted Rosie, tossing a strawberry felt marker onto the table.

Stefan kept pressing buttons. "And the year after that, two thousand, five hundred spiders. That's over a quarter million spiders in two years."

"I'd better get onto naming them," said Rosie. "Let's see. Brad, Jamie, Keanu...wait a minute, where's the father of Divana's babies?"

"I have not seen other spider around," Baba replied. "She leave him behind because looking for better husband. Not so bad idea. In meantime, she going to look after..."

"A quarter million babies in two years, " Rosie interrupted. "That's one heck of a lot of diapers."

"*Matka Bojha*! Mother of God," said Mom. "We are not buying them diapers. Can't you take up a more appropriate interest than spiders, for goodness sakes?"

"Babe, I think a sense of humour may be useful here," said Dad.

Mom placed her head against his shoulder. "I'll try, but

honestly!"

"Imagine fitting each diaper over eight legs," said Stefan. "Let's see. A quarter million times eight is..."

Baba spoke up. "This make me tired. What difference how many number spiders make? Is like try to count angels. Only is important spider eternal," she said. "Come on kids, we make nice spider kutya now."

She bustled into the kitchen. Rosie and Stefan followed close behind, reciting spider names.

"Buick!"

"Angelina!"

"Pontiac!"

Baba opened her special cupboard. Dad had built her a free-standing oak cabinet. The shelves were spaced so she didn't have to bend and stretch too much, as the arthritis in her knees was quite painful.

The cabinet held dozens of jars and paper bags filled with mysterious substances. There were green jars and blue jars filled with odd shapes, some sloshing in liquid. Small crumpled bags sat beside larger ones, rounded with their contents. The fragrance was like a rain forest, complete with wild mushrooms (of which there was a jar), crossed with a chemistry lab. It smelled really really good and really really terrible, all at the same time. Once it hit your nose, you couldn't stop sniffing. Secretly, Rosie thought that made it a lot like her family's armpits.

Baba reached into the cabinet, muttering to herself, "Wheat, poppy seed, crushed bug," and took out a pound bag of wheat berries. "Here, Rosie, you take bag. Pour one cup into big bowl and pour water on top. We make enough for everybody for tomorrow night dinner."

"I am *not* eating crushed bugs," Rosie declared, hands on her hips.

"Why not?" asked Stefan. "If they're good enough for Divana, they're good enough for us. Bugs have an incredibly high protein content. Mmmmm-MMMMMM."

"That's right," said Mom, picking at some purple grapes on the dining room table. "I prefer beetles with a little Tabasco sauce. There's a lovely 'squooooosh' in your mouth before the heat goes up your nose."

Dad smirked at her.

"What?" she said. "You told me to grab a sense of humour."

"Hmmmm. Give me fat juicy flies," Stefan replied. "Make sure you leave the wings on, because I like the crunch."

"Eeeeeewwwwwwwww!" said Rosie.

"You people disgusting," said Baba, shaking her head. "Rosie, we make kutya with wheat, honey and poppyseed for family. Only Divana get special crushed bugs. No honey, too sticky for spider."

"I thought we only ate kutya on Christmas Eve."

"Yes, that always part of Christmas. Because we use to call ancestors to come eat with us. We going to call ancestors to be with Divana, too. Anyway, wheat so healthy, is good to eat anytime. "

"You two sound like a Ukrainian commercial," said Stefan.

"Good!" Baba replied. "Is better kutya commercial, than terrible food they advertise in this country. Then they tell me, 'lick my finger'. I *poke* them with finger." She tickled Rosie's waist. "Better to eat healthy bug, any day." Rosie made a face.

Baba poured the poppy seeds into a small bowl to soak. Rosie followed suit with the wheat.

The next night after dinner, Rosie, Baba, Dad and Stefan gathered in Rosie's room. As often happened after a meal, Mom was in the bathroom. Rosie heard retching noises, then the toilet flushing. Dad shrugged and shook his head. Mom wordlessly put on a sweater and went out, slamming the door.

Divana was crouched on the edge of her web, the white ball on her stomach hanging comfortably over one of the strands.

Baba handed the cup of kutya to Rosie. "Here. You put one spoon in dirt on plant. She eat when she ready. Then you add fresh every day."

Rosie did. "Now what?" she asked.

"We say blessing for spider." Baba pulled out a stoppered bottle of slightly murky water. "Is from stream by my village," she explained.

"It's holy water, like the priest uses when we go to church," Rosie said.

"Don't need priest, don't need bless water. Water is already holy because is water," Baba replied. "Women been making protection with water in Ukraina fifteen thousand year. All you need do is say 'thank you' to One, She who create everything."

"Then why do we go to church *sometimes*?" Rosie asked.

"There are many ways for the Creator to love us, Rosie," Dad replied. "Church is a good place to meet neighbours and do community projects. That's how we love God back."

"Protecting animals is the best way to love God back," Rose replied.

"Is one of greatest way, for sure," said Baba. "And is most special way for you. You know this from time you born," Baba replied, then offered the jar to Rosie. She said, "Take little bit on fingers, and sprinkle toward web and plant. Tell Divana what you wish."

Rosie sprinkled the water, then said, "I want to do it silently." She closed her eyes and imagined the white silk ball on Divana's abdomen popping open easily, and hundreds of perfect, plump little spiderlings tumbling out. She saw them mimicking their mother's determined stride, her hunting stance, and the sweet way she waved her legs.

She felt a strong tug in her middle, and took a deep breath. The web she had sensed inside her when the family sang the Spider Song, spun out into an infinite universe. Beautifully marked Wolf spiders climbed spiral strands back and forth from coldly burning stars to the earth, creating galaxies as they went. Rosie was suspended in the Milky Way, her arms spread wide in deep blue space, stardust coating her in silvery, sparkling specks.

When she looked down on the planet, she saw infinite streams of reddish-yellow wheat, glossy vegetables and other good food making its way to people everywhere, down the silken strands. There was a golden rain of medicine for hurting creatures, too. She gathered some of its radiant warmth in her arms and tucked it inside her heart. *For when I need extra strength to heal an animal.*

Baba murmured in a soft, guttural voice, and sprinkled water towards Divana. Rosie shook her head and found herself back in the familiarity of her room.

Dad and Stefan sprinkled water as well. Stefan said, "Divana, I hope you have an easy time with your babies, and they all turn out healthy like you. And I'm sorry I said that about the Humane Society."

"Is good a blessing as any I ever heard," said Baba, smiling.

"Amen," said Rosie.

CHAPTER EIGHT

"Hey *spider girl!*" A wadded up paper ball hit Rosie's cheek. She spun around to see two girls standing at the lockers with Barb and Shelley. All four mouths turned up tightly, and their eyes held a hard glitter. Rosie held her head high and kept walking on shaky knees. Micheline was reaching into her own locker across the hall, acting as if she hadn't heard. But she joined Rosie. In home room, two girls had exchanged the seats nearest Rosie's with Brad and Mark. And there was a big black X on the corner of her desk.

"Wow. I haven't seen X for cooties since I was seven," she said evenly. "Have the grade twos been using this room?"

"Alright Rosie!" said Stefan.

A loud whisper came from the back of the room. "Spider girl is *seriously* infected. And she's a fatty, too!"

Bursts of laughter came from several places.

Micheline had taken the seat at Rosie's right, but sat with hands folded on her desk, looking attentively at the blackboard. She blew a six inch blue bubble. Peggy and Aleisha gave Rosie pained looks. Aleisha snarled, "You're idiots," at the back row. Her gold hoop earrings flashed with the shake of her head. "I-di-ots," Peggy mouthed to Rosie.

Mark leaned over at her left. "You are so cool, Rosie," he said.

Brad turned from his seat in front of Micheline. "Those girls are jealous. First you're the bike ramp champion, now you've got the guts to keep a spider. You ride horses and sing, too. They *hate* you." He grinned and tapped the band logo on his black t-shirt. "Awesome. Boring people always hate cool ones. That's rock 'n roll."

His dark blue eyes were warm and swept Rosie's face with affection. Aleisha winked at Rosie, who looked puzzled.

Rosie frowned. "I don't get it. Why wouldn't they want to do this stuff *with* me, instead of making fun? I haven't snubbed them."

Stefan leaned forward, and his dark brown hair flopped over one eye. He put on a heavy Ukrainian accent and clacked his teeth just like Baba. "Rosie, this way of world. People like this called *banyak*, head empty like pot. Sometime they hollow whole way inside. They want what whole people have. But not want to work for this. They very scared, like little Soviet. They also saying you not 'feminine' because you know how to do all these thing."

Rosie smiled at Stefan's imitation, then wrinkled her forehead. She said, "I thought this was about Divana. What's being 'feminine' got to do with anything?" She scratched her knee through her new riding breeches. She'd been wearing them for three weeks straight, washing them lovingly by hand every few days.

"You *are* feminine," said Mark. "Those other girls are desperate to be so feminine."

"Um, Rosie," said Micheline. "I need to tell you something." She flushed the same hot pink as her cotton blouse and looked intently into Rosie's eyes. For the first time ever, her gum had attached itself to a lock of hair, and Michie rolled the mess between her fingers as she spoke.

"Barb and Shelley started talking behind your back way before this. They've made fun of me for doing bike sports with you. They called me your 'boyfriend.' The spider thing is just an excuse to hurt you."

Rosie shook her head. "You didn't tell me."

"Well, I said that, obviously, I'm a girl. But if I was a boy,

I'd be proud to be your boyfriend. That shut them up. I think they were ashamed."

"And?" said Rosie, crossing her arms.

"Michie, they're not ashamed. They're so dumb, what you said confused them," Brad interjected.

Micheline went on. "I didn't tell you because you like them so much. I was worried you'd think I was lying and cut me off. I'm *such* a coward. The day you walked in on us in the bathroom, they were saying I had to choose between you and them." She shifted her eyes to the right. "It felt like the dentist had filled my mouth with freezing. I couldn't say, 'I choose Rosie,' even though that's what I feel." She pressed her hand to her chest. "I'm sorry. I'm really sorry."

Rosie opened her mouth, a sympathetic look on her face. She just as quickly snapped it shut and put her expression in neutral. She wasn't ready to forgive betrayal just yet. Aleisha turned in her seat and glared at Micheline. "You *are* a coward. How does Rosie know she can trust you now?"

An eraser hit Rosie on the back of her head. She calmly picked it up and began to scrub at the X.

"Whoa," said Mark. "Ultimate coolness."

"I've got spider power," Rosie whispered from the side of her mouth.

"And I've got a problem with these fools," said Aleisha. "We don't take stuff like this in New Orleans."

She flung her empty red and black vinyl pencil case to the back of the room. It hit Barb on her pert snub nose, which twitched. She shrieked and dramatically clutched her face. The girls on either side of her leaned in and whispered. Shelley put the funky case in her purse.

"You didn't have to do that Aleisha," said Rosie.

"Oh yeah, I did. I've been wanting to *so* bad."

Aleisha reached over and swept the top of Micheline's desk. Pens, colored pencils and a make up compact filled her hands. "If you're really Rosie's friend, Michie, commit yourself. Look innocent, y'all."

She glanced at the clock, counted to five, then flung the implements at the mean girls. Micheline's powder compact shattered against the back wall. Just as the back row began barraging the small group of friends with missiles, the teacher walked in.

"Cut it out!" she yelled. "Detention, all of you in back."

"Ma'am, oh ma'am?" Aleisha widened her eyes and waved her hand in the air.

The teacher, a former social worker, was overly solicitous of the New Orleans evacuee. "Yes dear?"

Aleisha's accent thickened. "Them girls in the back took my new pencil case. Said I was prob'ly ILL-litrit anyway. It's in that skinny rabbity-face one's purse."

Rosie and Micheline nodded 'yes.'

"Double detention," replied the teacher. "Up here please, Shelley."

When the bell sounded, Rosie and her friends gathered in the hallway. "Gee, Aleisha, I don't know if that was fair..." Rosie began, then burst out laughing. She clutched her stomach.

"I liked it," said Micheline, smiling. "But you owe me some make up, Aleisha."

"No, sweet thing. You're the one who owes someone something. That lame 'sorry' after what you said to Rosie? Huh."

The mean girls swept past, their faces twisted.

"Gotta work that liberal guilt," said Aleisha. "In this world, you gotta work everything. Nothing's fair. Come on Rosie. Let's get to band rehearsal. You taught us the Spider Song. Today I'm going to teach you *Everything I Do Gonna Be Funky From Now On*. We dance to it back home."

The rehearsal started right there in the hallway, with Rosie clapping and repeating the lines Aleisha started. It didn't take her long to pick up the strutting dance steps that went with the Allen Toussaint song.

Rosie mulled over the mean girl incident for the rest of the week. The web inside her that reached out so freely to the world, took on a protective coating. She could see out through the semi-transparent glaze, but not everyone was allowed to see in.

CHAPTER NINE

"I need a new hair style," Rosie said to Baba, tugging on her long, thick braid.

"Sure thing. Your hair start to look like hippie-shmippie."

"I want my hair ironed straight, and dark streaks in it. I feel really lame wearing this braid all the time."

"I just thinking make braid little tiny bit shorter. This style make you look like nice Ukrainian girl."

Rosie crossed her arms and stuck out her jaw. "Fine. Then I'm getting a belly button ring."

"Okay, okay, I pay for any haircut you want," said Baba. "You have cash for streak?"

"Of course," said Rosie. "I haven't bought a CD or *anything* for months. You'll have to lend me the money for the piercing, though."

"Not happening," Baba replied. "Day I lend money put hole in your *poopitz* is day I put rose on Stalin grave."

Rosie glared.

Baba ignored the look and continued, "Come on Rosie, my friend at best beauty salon in town know what to do. They very fashionable and they give you big deal on hair."

The beauty salon was just a few blocks away. Rosie outlined the possibilities for her hair as they walked. "I love reverse streaking. I want most of it burgundy, with a bit of dark copper."

"Not to be worry, Rosie," said Baba. "We make you look

like regular Miss America."

"No way. She looks phoney," said Rosie. "She has to smile all the time. I want to look like Birdy." She pulled a magazine photo from her shoulder bag.

"Birdy, Birdy," Baba replied. "That Ukrainian name? I bet is really 'Birdchuk'."

The salon looked well lived in. There were women under cone-shaped hairdryers along one wall, reading colourful magazines. Their heads were full of curlers and tin foil. Six hairdressers were cutting and blow drying hair at their stations. The receptionist gave Baba a cup of tea and Rosie a soft drink.

Rosie looked around at the salon. There were mirrors everywhere. Colourful mobiles hung from the ceiling, which had been painted to look like the sky, complete with fluffy clouds. The front window was filled with plants and rhythmic music blared from speakers.

"Ah, is Old Country glamour queen come visit us," called a stout woman with curly hair in a bright shade of red. "And is granddaughter here for more beauty too?" She put her scissors down and walked over to Baba and Rosie.

Baba whispered in the woman's ear. "Okay," the hairdresser said. "We make special cut and streak for pretty Rosie. I have new natural colour, not smell bad."

"Is it tested on animals?" asked Rosie.

"No!" said the hairdresser firmly, "This is a cruelty-free salon."

She showed Baba and Rosie to two chairs, side by side, and put a smock over Baba's dress. "First I ask Baba what she want, because her hair take longer. Then we do special for you, Rosie," she explained.

"Make me look like that Lady Goo Goo," Baba instructed, removing her babushka. "Lots fluffy hair."

"Is no problem," said the hairdresser.

"And make sure is Ukrainian red blondie, like little bit sunset on wheat," Baba added.

"Are you getting a belly button ring, too, Baba?" asked

Rosie hopefully.

"Ha! Would need six ring," said the hairdresser. Baba gave her a dirty look in the mirror, then smiled.

"You see. I do hair, then get handsome boyfriend," said Baba, folding her hands in her lap. "If Divana can get, I can get."

"You're lots prettier than Divana, Baba," said Rosie with a dismissive gesture. "She has eight legs and fly breath, too."

"Not to mention hairy back," replied Baba. "But that not stop her from getting boyfriend. It not stop hairdresser, either."

The hairdresser whacked Baba on the back of her head with a brush. "Ow!" said Baba, "Stop it. You disturb my glamour." She patted her curls.

"Who this Divana?" asked the hairdresser. "She sound like poor thing."

"Divana is our lucky spider," said Rosie proudly. "I rescued her from the cold, and she's already found us a farm and horses."

"We have lucky spider in salon, too," said the hairdresser. "Can you see?"

Rosie looked around. "No, I don't think so."

Baba laughed and said, "You see anything shape like spider, Rosie?"

Rosie looked again, carefully. "The chandelier has eight legs."

"That's right," replied the hairdresser. "Health department won't allow us keep spider web. I don't know why, spider cleaner than people. But chandelier also called *pavuk*, bring good luck here."

"Canada crazy. Health department, pah!" said Baba. "Kid wipe noses on bus seat, but I no can take clean animal on bus. In Ukraina, I take goat on bus all time. She sleep in house, too."

Rosie swung her chair back and forth with one foot. She looked at their reflections in the big salon mirror. "You took your goat on the bus?" she asked. "No way."

She used what she thought of as her "make Baba tell stories" voice. Innocent and sincerely enthusiastic. She enjoyed not only listening, but retelling the stories to her friends.

"Sure thing, Rosie," Baba replied. "Her name Sonia, short for *soniashnyk*, sunflower. I call her that because she follow patch of sun around all day, lie in it. Oh, she love that. You know how sunflower follow sun with their face? Sonia have very good suntan. Every day I put little bit suntan oil on her so she get brown faster. She start summer all white, and by end summer, she be dark like raisin." Baba put her hands over her heart. "She *dorahenka*, very dear goat."

The hairdresser rolled her eyes.

"I thought too much sun was bad for your skin," said Rosie. "You dragged me home early from the beach last summer, when all I wanted was a good tan."

"Only now, Rosie, with ozone layer doing bad thing," said Baba. "Long time ago, we stay in sun all time. Sonia like her tan very much. She come in house at night, first thing she do is look in mirror. She turn like this, like that. She look over her shoulder and smile at reflection."

The hairdresser bubbled air through her lips as she combed. "Your Baba buy goat bikini, too," she said.

"Don't you go make things up," said Baba, wagging her finger at the mirror. "That not true. Goat prefer naked when we home alone. But when company come, she put on very smart one piece. Bright red, with big yellow poke dot. Sonia fashionable kind of goat. Only thing too bad, she not smell so good like she look."

"Yes, smell is called 'bane of goat existence,'" the hairdresser said blandly. "Otherwise, they all be fashion model."

Rosie widened her eyes and crossed her fingers behind her back. "Did you get sunglasses for her too, Baba?"

"Oh yes. I make deal on black market. She have google kind. I wrap round head with elastic. She especially wear when she float on her back in pool."

"Oy, enough! We neighbour in Old Country," said the hairdresser. "You so poor like me, never had running water. We talk every day at village pump. Never mind swimming pool, you crazy woman."

"That because I keep secret place in woods," Baba replied smugly. "I make dam stream with log, and have pool. You never go that far for walk. You too lazy. I even make jacuzzi for Sonia."

Rosie tilted her head. "How did you make a jacuzzi in a stream?" she asked.

"With eggbeater, Rosie," said Baba. "Also very good exercise for upper arm. I best looking girl in village, wearing sleeveless. Your mother paying for aerobic. Ha! All she need is goat."

"I'll tell her that, Baba," said Rosie, grinning. "We can have goats at the new farm. I want one of those kind with the floppy ears. They're called Nubians."

"They very cute, Rosie," said Baba, "But you have to be careful what kind goat you get. Floppy-shmoppy ear get caught in jacuzzi. Very painful to pull out." She grimaced.

"So I've heard, Baba," replied Rosie. "It's in the 'caution' section of my goat keeping book."

Baba shot her a sideways glance.

Another hairdresser walked up and began playing with Rosie's hair. She was tall and slim, and wore many gold chains, which settled in the brown wrinkles of her neck. Her blonde hair was in an elaborate upsweep.

"I remember your Baba from village, too, Rosie. You look very much like her when she was little girl," she said. "Only I think you smarter."

"She smarter than all of us," Baba replied.

"I love these stories," the blonde hairdresser continued. "Rosie, she talk all time like this back home, too. No matter how hungry or how scared we get of Russian or Nazi soldier, your baba make us laugh like crazy people. Then we forget little bit how terrible things are."

"That very true," said Baba's hairdresser.

"That's good," Rosie replied. "I'm going to have lots of stories to tell people, too. I'll be a veterinarian *and* a comedian."

Baba smiled.

"Come on, you old glamour queen," said Baba's hairdresser. "First we wash hair, then we make you fluffy like this Lady Goo Goo."

Rosie could hear her baba and the hairdresser bantering down the hall. The words "jacuzzi", "crazy", and "bikini" floated back to her. She lifted her chin and told her own hairdresser, firmly, what she wanted done.

CHAPTER TEN

Rosie sat cross legged on her bed with a drawing pad in her lap and poked through a jar of coloured pencils. Photos her mom had taken of the new farm were spread across the bed. Her red gold hair was smooth. Burgundy streaks shimmered underneath, dyed with vegetable henna. The straightening had lengthened it, so it had gone from being just below her shoulder blades to nearly touching her waist.

The long strand by Rosie's left cheek flopped forward, obscuring her vision. She blew it away with a sideways breath. When that didn't work, she flipped it back dramatically and laughed. *Now I'm more 'feminine' than I ever wanted to be.*

She walked to the closet singing, "Look at me, I'm a super model," and took her black bike helmet from the shelf. She practiced stuffing her slippery new hair inside. She managed to get the back and right side in, but the left fell out. She tucked it in, and the back tumbled free. After several tries, she got all the hair neatly put up. *The braid was more convenient, for sure. Not that I'll ever admit it to Baba.*

She looked down at Divana, who was rummaging by the closet door. "Hmmm. I wonder if you're building a nest. Well, just put it where I can find it when we move."

Rosie's hair finally stayed put under the helmet. She picked up an umber pencil and made a few practice sketches with quick strokes. She put the pad down and counted on her fingers, "Micheline, Aleisha, Brad, Peggy, Mark, Barb, Stefan, Shelley. Oh, no."

Rosie's heart lurched painfully and her breathing quickened. She obviously couldn't invite Barb and Shelley. It was hard to adjust to losing friendships that had been going strong since grade one.

Rosie shut her eyes tight and imagined the coating on her web. Next, she activated the glowing Protection Dial in her chest. She reached up and gave it a good crank to the left, so it went from reading *Wide Open* to *Guarded But Willing to Forgive. Some Day.*

She folded six sheets of textured coloured paper in half. On the front of each, she sketched a picture of the family's new house, Billie, Jessie, and the two bantam chickens.

She wrote, "We're moving" across the top. Inside, she drew a picture of Divana hanging from a thread and holding a sign saying, "Come to our housewarming party", with the date and time, two Saturdays after moving day. She was making the invitations well ahead of time, so her friends knew she wasn't going to forget about them. "Bring your grandmas to party with mine," she added at the bottom.

As Rosie drew, she thought about the day before, when her family had visited the farm again. After her third riding lesson and many practice rides, Mrs. McIvor had invited her over to ride Jessie. She trembled all the way there in the car, and Baba patted her arm. "I think, Rosie, this Jessie be one those very special horse for you. You will have more than one, and you never forget them. Is good thing to love so much."

There were four people squished together in the back seat. Dad had installed an extra set of seat belts, just to drive Rosie and Baba's friends around. Peggy listened quietly, leaning against Rosie in the back seat. Aleisha sat erect, her keen eyes taking in every sight around her. It had taken her some time to become interested in anything since she arrived in Vancouver after evacuating New Orleans, and Rosie was glad to see the change.

Rosie gave Mrs. McIvor a drawing of Divana. "Isn't she lovely?" was her response. "I like the way you've shown her distinct markings. Is she really this hairy?"

"Is scout honour," said Baba, holding up her hand. "She look like woolly thing."

"She's a Wolf spider," said Rosie proudly, "She'll probably have her babies right here on the farm. Maybe as many as three hundred. You should see the huge white egg case on her tummy. She sounds like a horse when she walks."

"Isn't that wonderful!" replied Mrs. McIvor. "I wish her a healthy time of it, and many, many lovely babies."

"Me too," said Peg.

"Yes ma'am. My grandma says she's gonna have as many babies as Anansi the Spider's wife," said Aleisha.

"Dear God. You're all in on it," said Mom.

Mrs. McIvor led Billie and carefully supervised Rosie as she brought Jessie in from pasture. "There's a correct way to lead a horse through a gate, dear. I want to make sure you and the horses are safe."

Rosie unlatched the gate with Jessie held firmly to her right side, then bumped it with her hip. When the gate was fully open, she led Jessie through. She kept control of the little mare's feet at all times, not allowing her to barge ahead. At the same time, Rosie kept an eye on Billie, who was just a few feet behind Jessie. She swung the gate shut in time to keep Billie in the pasture.

"Perfect," said Mrs. McIvor. She latched the gate and gave Billie a gentle pat on his soft white nose.

When they got to the barn, the little red chickens went hop! hop! hop! from floor to hay bale to the horses' backs, fluffed their feathers and nestled down. The horses were clearly used to the chickens' company, as they didn't flinch.

"Aren't they the *dearest* things," said Mom, clasping her hands. Dad rubbed her back. "I'm glad you're getting pets, too. Personally, I think I'll give that big chestnut fella a try. He really is a lot like old Bosco."

"But no beer for horse," Baba said firmly. "If I have to tell you again, I stop brewing."

"Mama, I am fifty years old, and I don't need to be told to not give beer to my horse," he replied. "I didn't even know what beer was, back then. I just thought that if Dad liked it as a treat, so would Bosco."

"My grandma would love that story," said Aleisha.

Rosie groomed Jessie until her coat shone like black glass, and lifted the saddle onto her back. The black mare shuddered and tossed her head when Rosie drew the girth. Peggy and Aleisha had been stroking her neck, and they stepped away.

Rosie froze. Mrs. McIvor spoke. "You haven't done anything wrong, dear. It's just that Jessie sometimes gets unsure with sudden movements. I should have told you to give her a rub in the girth area before buckling up."

"Shhhhh girl," said Rosie as she quickly unbuckled and massaged the delicate skin behind the mare's elbows. Jessie took a huge breath, turned to look at Rosie, then exhaled and relaxed, her nostrils fluttering. Rosie drew the girth smoothly. Jessie stood like a rock.

"Beautiful!" said Mrs. McIvor.

Mom's grip on Dad's arm loosened. "Will she buck?" asked Dad.

"Never. She has no bad memories of anyone on her back, so she's perfectly confident with a rider. She only occasionally reacts to movements that remind her of babyhood mistreatment."

The three girls went into the tack room, where it took Peggy and Aleisha a good five minutes, giggling and whispering, to tuck Rosie's new hair under a velvet hard hat. "Your hair looks awesome, Rosie," said Aleisha, "But it's not exactly convenient for an athlete. I'm going to give you hairstyling lessons. You're gonna have a real cool do."

"That would be amazing," Rosie replied.

"In exchange for drawing lessons," added Aleisha.

"That's an easy price," said Rosie.

"The helmet buckle was stiff," Peg said to the group when

they finally emerged.

They walked to the grassy ring beside the barn. Rosie mounted expertly, and asked for a walk. She squeezed her calves a little with each stride, as the coach had shown her. She thrilled at the sight of Jessie's long, dark mane rippling as she moved. This was better than Rosie's wildest fantasies.

"Good," said Mrs. McIvor. "You know how to make a horse step out. Now hold the reins like they're silk threads. Softly, softly. You should be able to feel the horse's mouth."

Rosie focused intently on the feel of the supple leather in her hands. She breathed deeply. As she did, it suddenly felt as if the reins really *were* threads, flowing from the ends of her fingers. She could feel Jessie's mouth quivering along the strands. "Oh!" she said, "I know what you mean. It's like the way Divana's web moves just slightly when she walks on it."

"Yes, Rosie! That's exactly it. You have the feel of a real horsewoman. It's called 'soft hands.'"

"I'm going to close my eyes for a while" Rosie said. "That's what works when I plan my next move on my bike."

"I've never heard anyone say that before, but that's fine. Stay at a slow walk along the long line of the fence. I'll tell you to open them when you're four steps from the corner."

Rosie closed her eyes, and Jessie kept moving forward, her back swinging. The web inside spun outwards again, and Rosie saw herself join the ranks of horsewomen before her. First hundreds, then thousands of women with sure seats and soft hands, riding the spiral strands of the web. They sat astride blacks, bays and chestnuts, and all shades in between.

All sizes, too, from the smallest Caspian ponies to the largest draft horses. Joan of Arc was there, defending France in shining armour on her mighty war horse. So was Lady Godiva, who rode naked and brave through the streets of Coventry to protest her husband's cruelty.

Their horses pranced with knees high and cantered with thunderous majesty. Baba and her Misha were there, too, galloping joyfully along a glowing thread, before the Soviets cast suspicion on women's healing powers and stole the white mare away.

Rosie felt Jessie's soft mouth in her hands, and they talked to each other through the reins. She suddenly knew it had been this way between people and horses since her Ukrainian ancestors, the Scythians and Amazons, first tamed them and rode side by side with their men. There may have been thousands of years between, but on the spokes of Rosie's web, they all existed at once. Riders and horses, each pair deep in private conversation.

Rosie sighed, and felt Jessie's skin quiver beneath her.

"The corner's coming!" called Mrs. McIvor.

Rosie snapped to attention and guided the mare into the curve with legs and hands. She trotted the in circles, then cantered in both directions. It was like riding a cloud.

"Very nice, dear," said Mrs. McIvor after Rosie halted in the centre of the ring. She patted her leg. "I feel confident leaving Jessie and Billie in your care. Don't be afraid to ask your coach questions, or to give me a call in Ontario, either."

"Is Jessie so sensitive to ride because of her background?" asked Rosie.

"Partly, dear. But mainly, she's an exceptional mare. She has repaid me many times over in the years since I rescued her."

"Is trade off, Rosie," Baba added. "Just like immigrant from bad situation. He have trouble, but also deeper and more feeling inside."

"Yes," said Mrs. McIvor. "Where would our country be without immigrants?"

Aleisha looked down at her hands, her forehead wrinkling. "What if we don't really want to be here?" she mumbled.

"What if I told you how much we want you here?" Rosie replied.

The group sat down to tea in the living room. Mrs. McIvor had prepared a piping hot pot with real tea leaves, as well as homemade scones and raspberry preserves.

She stood up, cup in hand, and pointed out the side

window.

"Over to the west is the Stewart farm. They're organic gardeners, and will be happy to exchange information and plants with you."

"Behind us, to the north, is the Didichuk place," the lady continued. "The gentleman of the family is also very good with tools."

"I already met Mr. D at the Co-op Store," said Dad. "He offered to help me set up my tool shed."

Baba said, "Didichuk. This Ukrainian name. Good! I go meet as soon we move. I bet they have decent dill weed for my borshch. Last time I have to use some dry nonsense from shaker because too much rain kill our real thing. It taste like straw. Pah! I spit on it."

"I know what you mean," said Mrs. McIvor. "I can't bear herbs from the store, either. I'm sorry, I have no dill, but you'll find some beautiful rosemary, mint and lemon balm out in the garden."

Aleisha piped up. "My grandma says the same kinds of things about bland food on the West Coast, compared to Louisiana."

"Never mind. I cook your grandma food, blow top her head off," said Baba.

"She'll probably say the same thing about her own cooking to you," said Aleisha in a teasing tone. "Wait till you taste her homemade hot sauce. She makes one *mean* gumbo." She fanned herself.

"Rosie, why all your friend so big mouth?" asked Baba, taking a second spoonful of raspberry preserves.

Rosie bit her tongue. "Any neighbours with kids?" she asked.

"Yes, dear, the Zastres across the road have twins about your age." She gestured at the plate glass window with a scone that dripped butter. "A boy and a girl. They also love horses, and are quite good with them."

"What kind of horses?" asked Rosie.

"Let's see. Christopher has a bay Quarter Horse, and

Leanne, a Thoroughbred/Paint cross. She looks something like Jessie, if you threw a bucket of white paint over her."

"Great! We can go riding together," she said through a mouthful of crumbs.

Rosie looked at Aleisha and Peggy hopefully. "Are you guys going to learn to ride?"

"Uh, noooooo," Aleisha replied. "Horses are pretty and everything, but I like solid ground."

Peggy shook her head 'No.' "But I can show you some moves I learned on the 'horse' in gymnastics club," she said, positioning her arms above her head.

"That's cool," Rosie replied. Maybe I'll learn flying dismounts, too. Then Michie and I can....oh." She swallowed and turned to Mrs. McIvor. "Are Chris and Leanne in 4-H or Pony Club, so they can show me the ropes?"

"I believe Chris is in 4-H, because he prefers to ride Western, and Leanne rode in Pony Club with my grandchildren. It's up to you Rosie, because Jessie and Billie are trained both ways."

"They trained like Cossack horse?" asked Baba, lifting her chin.

"That would be amazing," said Rosie.

"Well, I don't know if any horses in Canada are trained *that* well," replied Mrs. McIvor. "After all, the Cossacks' horses are expected to keep a rider safe in battle, just like the Lippizzan stallions."

"Is true!" said Baba. "Army of Cossack defeat Nazi soldier in tank regiment during war. I see this. Those horse fearless." She leaned forward and gestured as if she was following a horse's surging head with the reins. Tea sloshed onto the lap of her skirt. Rosie quickly sponged the fabric with her napkin, spilling crumbs on both Baba and the rug. Peggy gently dabbed the old woman's socks.

Mom put her head in her hands.

"Hmmmm," said Mrs. McIvor, acting as if she didn't notice. "I don't think you'd see that in Canada. But I can tell you that Jessie doesn't mind my granddaughter standing straight up on his back at a canter!"

"I'm going to do that," said Rosie. "By the end of this summer."

"I'm sure you will, dear. And who do you think showed my granddaughter how?" The old lady's eyes twinkled.

"Too bad you not staying in BC," Baba said to Mrs. McIvor, shaking her head. "You and me, we could make old age pension riding show. Take to *National Exhibition Pacific* and make lots money. I wear red satin pant and beautiful embroider blouse, braid ribbon in horse mane."

Mrs. McIvor nodded. "Yes, we could. I'd wear my clan tartan, and the same for my horse's saddle blanket."

Baba said, "We could have old age women from all country in their good clothes, all ride together! Why should musical ride RCMP have all fun? Every time I see them, I yell," she put down her tea and cupped her hands around her mouth. "'Put down those spear and fight with bare hand, like real man!'"

"She also wolf whistles through her fingers at them," said Rosie. She demonstrated. Everyone in the room clapped their hands over their ears at the shrill sound.

"Rosie..." Dad began.

"Hee hee," went Aleisha.

Rosie ignored them. "Then we go back to the stables, and Baba tells the officers how handsome they are."

"Oh oh oh," said Aleisha, clutching her stomach. "It hurts." She squinched her eyes shut.

Baba flashed her a filthy look.

Peggy studied her hands. Mrs. McIvor gazed seriously at Rosie. Mom just sat quietly.

Rosie continued, enjoying the effect she was having. "Once, one of them said," she stood up, placed hands on hips, her feet wide apart, and put on a deep, authoritative voice, "'Ma'am, if you weren't so obviously harmless, we'd consider you a security risk.'"

"Who harmless?" Baba asked indignantly, leaning forward.

"Not you, Mama," said Dad.

"Oh no, not you, dear," said the Scottish lady. "He was flirting."

"Yes Baba, he was flirting. He was admiring a woman with a real personality," Rosie added.

"That's right," said Mom.

Baba sat back, hands folded snugly across her belly. "I think so. Was right after I make fluffy hair at salon."

Aleisha stumbled to the bathroom, thighs pressed tightly together. "Oh oh OH," echoed down the hall.

The family bid a fond farewell to Mrs. McIvor, promising to write or call if they had any questions about the farm. She'd given Rosie a warm hug and pressed something into her hand.

CHAPTER ELEVEN

In the back seat with Baba, Aleisha and Peggy, Rosie displayed the object on her palm. It was a blue horse show ribbon, folded neatly. It sprung open, revealing a ceramic medal in the centre with an ink outline of a leaping horse over the word 'First.'

"What did she say to you, Rosie?" asked Aleisha, breathless. She had been last to the car.

"Until you start winning your own," Rosie answered.

"Good!" said Baba. "Soon we move, I start your training. I take my riding pant to dry cleaner yesterday. Have kutya stain. Also please remind me, I need stronger glue for false teeth. Not want them fall out when I pick up handkerchief."

"No, we sure don't want that," said Dad from behind the wheel. He gave his head a shake, then he and Mom resumed their conversation.

"Excuse me?" asked Aleisha. Rosie explained, and the three girls quickly looked in different directions. Each time their eyes slid towards each other, one of them would start to giggle. Peggy pulled the neck of her t-shirt up over her mouth, which, Rosie didn't mind saying, caused her to look like a turtle and made matters worse. Finally, Peg started to hiccup from the effort of restraining herself. Baba clapped her on the back while Rosie yelled, "Boo!"

The hiccups stopped, but not before Peg let out a loud burp.

"Between you, me, and bedpost, Pegichka, you need learn be little more self control in public," said Baba. The girls exploded with laughter.

They got a grip and sat silently for a while. Now and then, one of them shook a little.

Then Rosie said, "Baba, I want to tell you something." She related the sensations and vision she'd had on Jessie's back. The exquisite feel of the delicate mouth along the strands of the reins, the generations of horsewomen riding the spiral.

Baba looked sharply sideways at Rosie, as if examining her. "You been seeing this web all along, Rosie?"

"Yes. Ever since Divana came. It started when you sang the Spider Song. When I'm on a horse, it's intense."

She placed both hands on her belly. "I can feel this strong tug in my middle, as if I'm tied to somewhere way out in the universe, at the same time I'm anchored to the horse's centre. She looked anxiously at Baba. "I feel weird saying it out loud."

Aleisha placed both hands on her own belly and slowly moved her head to the left as if listening to something far away. Peggy cautiously followed suit.

"No, no," said Baba, patting Rosie's arm. "Is gift. You seeing how Baba Spider keep weaving world. She talk to people in different way, Rosie. Only with you, I think is very direct because you know how to listen to animal. World is weaving not only outside, but inside us, too. Many people not look that deep. Or that far. You lucky."

Rosie let out a long breath. "That's good, because I thought I was hallucinating or something."

Peggy shifted in her seat and moved her head in the other direction. Aleisha listened intently to the conversation.

"No, Rosie," Baba replied. "Is very real, what you see. Jewish scientist name Einstein even prove, say 'all time relative.'" She made a large gesture with her hands. "That mean everything happen all at once. Then scientist name Stephen Hawking talk about imaginary time. It have all direction, and no direction, all at once.

Time and history just like Divana web. It live in spiral, no beginning and no end. Time not happen in straight line, boom boom boom! But Rosie, only few people strong enough to see what Einstein mean, inside yourself. You probably feel like something inside spinning, too?"

"Yes!" Rosie felt startled, then relieved. "Do you know what I mean?"

"Run in family, sweetheart, run in family," said Baba, her hand still on Rosie's arm. "Is how feel to be powerful woman."

Baba took a scrap of paper and a pen from her purse and drew. The girls leaned over to look. "You see spiral?" Baba asked. "I draw this on pysanky, along with web. Ukrainian women, they put spiral on egg for, oh, maybe fifteen, twenty thousand year now."

"I've seen that design on African fabric," said Aleisha. "Here, I'll draw it for you."

She took the pen from Baba and drew a spiral with what looked like teardrops at the ends of the lines.

"I'm not surprise," said Baba. "Is where we all come from, in first place. Then people migrate to Ukraina through Middle East. Some not even stop, just get more pale from weak sun." She put her hand on her belly. "Older you get, stronger feeling is. All universe contain in here. Belly button, is where woman really see from, as well as eyes."

Rosie pressed her left hand to her own belly and closed her eyes. She glimpsed the spiral universe, sparkling with prismatic colours. The hues were rich and transparent at once, and pulsed gently with her heartbeat. Peggy moved her hands so her thumb was over her belly button. "Oh my!" she said.

"Yes, Baba, I see just as well from there, as from my eyes," said Rosie.

"Me too," said Aleisha. "But I *feel* it, more than actually seeing."

Mom turned around, her glasses down at the end of her nose. "I don't 'see' a blessed thing," she said. "All that matters is that my belly stays empty and flat."

Baba looked at her with soft eyes and grunted, then turned

back to the girls.

"But be careful how you tell people these things yet, maybe. They funny about these sort thing. Okay for girl to run round with belly button hang out, underwear like dental floss, leak her power everywhere like bad broken tap. But talk about women have big universe power in belly, pow! people get mad."

"Why is that, Baba?" asked Peggy.

Baba sighed. "Because see girl running round naked make man happy, but big power in belly belong only to woman. In Canada, this not allowed. Woman not allowed to have woman secret, everything belong to men. Then they make you crazy by say 'equal right', but you not have that, no way. Enough to make woman go out from her rocker."

Aleisha nodded. "I know exactly what you mean, Baba. It's like the girls at school who talk toughest about how ridiculous boys are, wear the most revealing outfits. Or, like those girls who hate Rosie because she knows she can do anything a boy can."

Rosie hung her head. "But it hurts that Barb and Shelley hate me so much. Isn't there anything I can do?"

Peggy inhaled deeply and said, "I don't think so, Rosie. Sorry."

"Uh uh uh, noooooo," Aleisha confirmed. "When people are that insecure, any steps you take toward them gives them more opportunities to attack you. Besides," she added with a cheerful grin, "You've got us."

Rosie felt a thrill in her heart. The glass splinters from Micheline's and the other girls' betrayals began melting into a rounded shape.

Baba said, "Girls so confused. They told they powerful and equal. Some them, like these girls feel it, but not trained to use power to help themselves. It make me wild. In Ukraina, we not talk so much about this equal right."

Rosie startled. "Pardon?" she asked.

She rolled down the car window a bit further and breathed in the country air. "Everyone *know*, without woman power, whole world fall apart. Man very respected, but woman head of house and village. And way women attack women here when she show this inside power, make turn my stomach." She shook her head.

"I think equal rights are achieved through political action and intellectual conversation," said Mom. "Are you saying they can happen through some kind of belly mumbo jumbo and *physics*?"

"Yes, finest kind," Baba replied. "Rosie just figure out theory relativity, and I help her with equation."

Dad cut his eyes away from the road for a moment, glancing at Mom. "Mama used to try to get me and Uncle to study Einstein's theories. We didn't get it."

"That because only woman can understand," Baba humphed and folded her hands in her lap. "Actually invented by Mrs. Einstein, because she have spinning inside her too. She very connect to Baba Spider. I write with her, you know."

"Yes, I read that somewhere about Mileva Einstein," said Mom. "She gave up her brilliant career to have babies, though. How interesting that you corresponded."

"Is just another kind spinning of universe, making babies," said Baba. "Not matter if you publish paper or make painting or have children. You still inside spider web. You have to choose strong, which kind way the spinning go out into world. Important thing is, you not hold back, and you not do it for someone else. *That* make you crazy. You make decision to do what you want, and you stick to this. You don't be worry what other people say."

"I don't," Rosie replied. She adjusted the waistband of her charcoal breeches, now in their sixth week of wearing.

"Me neither," said Peggy. "I'm going to be a professional musician and have sixteen children."

"Not me, not ever," said Aleisha. "In fact, I'm going to study physics."

"That is good thing, Peggy and Aleisha," Baba replied. "Mrs. Einstein say I help her with theorem mathematical of relativity. Because I all time talking about spiral strand on

Hanya Oksanichka Sophia Slowka Alexandrichka web, how never begin or end."

"Baba," said Aleisha slowly, "When you say Mrs. Einstein, do you mean Albert's wife?"

"I saw the letters when we lived in Ukraine, Aleisha," said Dad from behind the wheel. "About once a month, for years, Mama would read her letters from Mileva Einstein out loud." Baba nodded. "I saved the Austrian stamps," Dad added.

"I think I would have liked Mrs. Einstein," said Rosie. "Maybe we would have gone horseback riding together."

"I think you would have like her very much, Rosie," Baba replied. "She especially mad at husband for letting this knowledge ancient turn into nuclear bomb, instead of keep for healing of people. She say 'Stop! Stop!' but nobody listen, because she woman."

"Well, I know how *I'm* going to use it," said Rosie.

"That's my girl," said Dad.

***

A knock on Rosie's bedroom door startled her from her reminiscence. She was abruptly back on her bed, with paper and colored pencils scattered around.

"Come in?" she said uncertainly.

Baba peeped in. "Why is thing on your head?" she asked, pointing.

Rosie's hands flew up and met hard plastic. Her eyes widened. "Um, it's my drawing helmet."

"I buy you nice hair band, sweetheart," said Baba, and winked.

CHAPTER TWELVE

Moving day came quickly. Boxes from the grocery, computer and liquor stores were piled in the living room and kitchen. It wasn't possible to open a closet without meeting a stack of boxes.

A week before the move, Rosie found Mom and Baba sweating in the June heat, wrapping dishes in the kitchen. "I'm making sure Divana gets to the new house safely," she said. She held up a small white box from the local Chinese restaurant. "It has the symbol for good luck printed on it, too."

"Divana will be take out," said Baba. "Spider Foo Young." She slapped her thigh at the joke.

Rosie stared at her. Baba continued,"Is real good box. Just put grass and drop of water night before. Is probably a good idea to slide spider in with piece of cardboard. Don't pick her up with your hands in case you break egg case."

"She's going to ride on my lap in the car, too," said Rosie. "Hey, wow, what if she has her *babies* in the *car*?" Mom rubbed her temples. She began to mutter, but Baba silenced her with a look.

The night before the move, Rosie only had a suitcase of clothes left to pack. All her books, games and ornaments were neatly put away in boxes that lined the bedroom walls. She sat on the bed, looking around. The only evidence that was left of her many pictures was dark spots on the walls, and a few stray pieces of tape. "Sure looks empty in here," she sighed. Her voice echoed. Baba knocked on the frame of the open door. "Can I come in?"

"Sure, Baba," Rosie answered. "I'm surprised I feel so sad. I've been so excited about the farm, I forgot how much I like living here."

"Yes," Baba said, "Is always hard to leave home." She sat down and put her arm around Rosie. "By way, where is that Divana? You should pack up before bedtime."

Rosie glanced up at the web. "I don't know," she said, "I haven't seen her all day." She jumped up to look more closely. Her movements grew abrupt as she brushed aside the leaves of her plants.

"She's not here." She pulled away the only thing left on her closet floor, an empty suitcase. "She's not in the closet, either." Her voice shook.

"Rosie, not to panic," said Baba. "Spider upset by all commotion in house. She just hiding little bit. We just make sure not to vacuum here until we find her."

Divana did not appear by bedtime. Rosie had a hard time falling asleep that night. She pictured the family turning into their new driveway and seeing the horses. She turned the white take out box in her hands. *Without Divana, our luck will disappear. What if the farm and horses disappear, too?*

She finally put the box on her bedside table, and drifted off in the wee hours.

And then it was time to move.

Rosie woke up with drool on her pillow and dark circles under her eyes. "Huh?" she grunted. She immediately looked up at the web. No Divana. She clutched the white take out box in one hand and balanced herself on the other and her knees. She limped into the closet like a lame horse.

The moving truck is coming. The voice in her head was panicky. *I still have to pack my clothes and vacuum. Where's Divana?* She plunked herself down in a corner of the closet.

"Why you hiding?"

Rosie jumped at the sound of Baba's voice, then said mournfully "Divana's missing. I'm not leaving without her.

Are you aware she's *pregnant*?"

"Hey, poopchik, no need for sarcastic. Here, let me look." Baba pushed all the plant leaves aside, but didn't find the spider. "Listen, sweetheart, she turn up," she said.

"And wouldn't Mom just love it if she didn't," Rosie said harshly.

"Not to be worry. Leave up to me. I convince her best thing for Divana and babies is to take to farm." Baba strode off.

Rosie stayed in the closet on her hands and knees. She poked morosely at a couple of t-shirts that had fallen off their hangers. *I'm pawing at grass under snow with my hoof.*

Baba returned with Mom.

"Darling," said Mom, a bit too sweetly. "If Divana doesn't show up before the truck comes, she'll be fine. The new people aren't moving in here for ten days. I promise we'll come back every day and look for her."

"I'm leaving plants on the sill, so she has a place to hunt bugs," said Rosie.

"We also leave vacuum here," added Baba, "So you don't have to use until we find spider."

"Fine," said Mom. Her voice was still sugary, but her lips pressed tightly against her teeth. Rosie had seen a llama do the same, right before it spit noxious green guck on a pestering child.

By the time the family had to follow the moving truck, Divana hadn't shown herself. Rosie sat silently in the back seat with Baba. The old woman muttered comforting words, but it didn't help the panic and emptiness inside her. Her parents' conversation made things worse.

"I can hardly wait to drive all the way back here in the *five minutes* I have between unpacking, gardening, writing my book and working at the store," Mom hissed to Dad. "Why couldn't I have a daughter who cares about fluffy kittens and ballet instead of spiders, bikes and horses?"

"I'm taking a few days off in the next couple of weeks, babe," he replied. "I have to set up my new workshop, anyway. Driving Rosie will be a nice break. Don't sweat." He patted Mom's knee.

"You're going along with this spider nonsense," said Mom.

"Not necessarily. I'm encouraging you to not make an enemy of our daughter," he said. "I sense there's a lot going on for her about this spider thing that's below the surface."

"You 'encourage' her fantasies," said Mom.

"Maybe you don't encourage them enough," Dad replied.

Rosie opened her mouth to speak. Baba placed a cautionary hand over Rosie's.

They think I'm hard of hearing. Rosie started. *Or maybe they want me to hear them.*

They reached the farm, and Rosie forgot her bad feelings for a while. She carried her suitcase into her new room, which was painted the colour of fresh cream. When she looked out the window, she could see Billie and Jessie with their heads hung over the pasture fence, watching the activity curiously. Her heart leapt. She went out to them, grabbing a few carrots Mrs. McIvor had left in the fridge. Jessie nickered when Rosie came out the back door, and Rosie's heart leapt.

Rosie spent a pleasant hour grooming the horses, shaking fragrant hay into their stalls and filling their water.

Baba came down for a few minutes, said, "Good job," and left Rosie to it. Rosie saddled Jessie and went for a ride along the pasture boundaries. After cooling her down and a quick brushing, she put her in her stall for the night. The last thing Mrs. McIvor had done before leaving was to put a scoop of oats in each manger; Rosie leaned on Jessie's stall for a while and listened to her munch, smiling. She kissed the horses' noses and went in the house.

Her bad feelings returned immediately. She pretended she was washing them off under the shower, like Baba had taught her, but they clung to her through dinner and a round of unpacking. When Rosie glanced up at the window in her new bedroom, the empty corner was like a punch to her stomach.

Even though she was very tired, she spent another sleepless night. She dreamed that Divana was trying to have her babies, but was lost in an endless, dark closet. She was rolling the egg case around because she could hear her babies pushing from the inside, trying to get out. But try as she might to open the case with her fangs and eight legs, it was useless. Jessie and Billie stood outside the closet, pawing and snorting in a menacing way, and the only source of light was the red glow of the chickens' eyes.

The next morning, she and mom drove back to the old house, picking up Aleisha on the way. Their footsteps echoed in the empty rooms. Still no Divana anywhere. On the ride back to the farm, Rosie twisted the blue seat cover between her fingers. "It's my fault," she said. "I should have looked for her and put her in the box earlier."

"When was the last time you saw her?" asked Aleisha, pulling the fabric away from Rosie's hand.

"About seven pm the night before we moved," she answered. "And when Baba and I looked again at nine, she was missing."

"You're mad at yourself for not guessing when she'd hide," said Aleisha. She arched an elegant eyebrow. "Is knowing how spiders tell time something I missed in *Life Skills* class?"

Rosie laughed, just a very little bit.

Two more days went by, with Mom or Dad driving Rosie back to look for Divana. By now, she was frantic. "She's gotten stuck in a crack in the wall with her egg case, or the movers stomped on her. I just know it," she moaned.

On the fourth day, Baba met Rosie and Dad at the door of the farmhouse. "Come here, I have something important show you," she said. Her face gave away nothing.

They followed her into the living room, where she pointed to the basket of pysanky. Rosie noticed something odd about the familiar stack of brightly coloured eggs. Something very odd. Baba put her hand to small of Rosie's back. "Go look. Be quiet, Rosie," she said.

Rosie looked. She blinked. Once, twice, then burst into

tears. Divana was sitting calmly on top of the red egg with the spider web design, her egg case now incredibly large. It looked ready to pop. Baba and Dad rubbed Rosie's back. She wiped her tears and said, "What a baby I am."

Mom heard Rosie crying, and joined the group.

"It's okay sweetheart," said Baba. "I want cry too. But look how much Divana need to be close to her ancestor history, to get ready to *make* baby."

Rosie took several deep breaths with her eyes closed, hand on her belly. She caught a glimpse of the vision she'd had when they were blessing Divana at the old house. For a few moments, she let herself again be lifted into a swirl of blue and silver galaxies and the rain of golden light.

"Yes, I can feel that," she said. A drop of the light coalesced into a sharp beam . It widened into a spotlight on Divana and the pysanky. Then part of it withdraw into Rosie's middle, where it hummed. "I think she's about ready to have her babies."

"Is good!" said Baba, "We light candle and wait up tonight, yes?"

"Rosie," said Mom, "It's time to decide what to do with the spiders. I am *extremely* upset." Her nails dug into her palms, and her knuckles whitened. Rosie focused on the lines on her mom's fingers, and then the spaces between the lines.

"We do need to make a plan, Rosie," said Dad.

Rosie drew herself up. The spiral web inside her gave a hard twist. Her soul was hot lava and undulating muscle. She suddenly felt, clearly and sharply, the imposing woman she would become. It was as if her adult self stood both inside and behind her like a spirit shadow, pushing her to create her own future.

Rosie pinned her mother with a level gaze. Her eyes sparkled and darkened. "How can I possibly know what their purpose is before they're even born?" she asked in a deep, throaty voice. "Doesn't the Spider Song mean anything real to you?"

She turned to Dad with the same strong, imperious look.

"Why even teach me that song unless it *means* something? Animals are not a joke to me."

"I can hear that," said Dad cautiously. He took a step back. His eyes flicked back and forth between Rosie and Mom.

Mom turned her head away. "I think I'll go calm myself," she said.

"Is good idea," said Baba, placing her hand on Mom's thin back. The entire curve of her shoulder blades showed through her blouse. "Time when baby being born is not time for bottom line. This serious spiritual business."

Mom left the room. Her bare feet made hard slapping sounds on the wood floor. Dad followed her, making soothing noises.

That night, Baba opened her special cupboard and took out two beeswax pillar candles. She handed them to Rosie, who held them up to her nose and inhaled deeply of the honey scent. They carried them into the living room, along with a jug of apple juice and a plate of cookies. She had not moved Divana to her new bedroom, as the little spider seemed content exploring the basket of pysanky and the living room plants.

Rosie and Baba sat down in two blue easy chairs, near the table with the basket. Baba put her feet up and opened an issue of *Popular Mechanics*. Rosie began reading *Son of the Black Stallion* for the third time. Around 2 am, Baba's head dropped to the side, and a light snore came whistling through her dentures. Rosie looked at her, smiled, and tried to keep reading. But the words on the page blurred, and soon she found her own head nodding. The last thing she saw was Divana, crouched on the rim of the basket.

In her dream, she was still in the living room with Baba. But the end wall had disappeared, and Divana sat at the centre of an infinite web stretched against a royal blue sky. Stars twinkled through the strands. She crooned to her babies, rocking the egg case in her front legs. The little spider's singing voice was sweetly husky:

Before there was a world
I was there
I was there
Weaving the stars together
I made a web where we could live

I will feed everyone
I bring my children
All good things.

To my children I bring three friends
The shining sun
The bright moon
And a light rain
So things can grow.

Weaving the stars together
I bring all good things
I bring all good things.

Mama Spider weaves the web of life
I give you the beauty of my designs
So we can all be together
We will be kind to each other
And our lives will be good luck.

Weaving the stars together
I bring all good things
I bring all good things.

When the world is no more
I will be there
I will be there for you
There is no end to this web
There is no end to time
No end to us.

Weaving the stars together
I bring all good things

I bring all good things.

Then Divana gently, very gently, inserted the tips of her fangs into the egg case, and pulled. The tiniest tear appeared in the white fabric. From it waved a leg thin and graceful as an eyelash. Then another. And another, until an entire baby spider tumbled out onto the pysanky. She was followed by a second, a third, and then a tidal wave of brothers and sisters, the tear widening as they tumbled through. Three dozen, six dozen, then dozens more, they kept pouring from the heavy white silk case.

Rosie had a strange, urgent feeling during the dream. She awoke with a jolt, eyes wide open. She looked at the basket and blinked at the designs on the pysanky. They wavered like a landscape seen through a heatwave. She blinked again. "Oh!" her hand flew to her mouth. "It's true! Look at Divana's babies!"

Baba shook her head and came instantly awake.

Dozens of tiny round brown bodies scampered and skipped across the eggs on impossibly delicate legs. On each of their backs was just a hint of the lovely pattern that would develop as they grew. They contrasted wonderfully with the rich reds, yellows, oranges and blues of the eggs. Divana perched on the thick rim of the woven basket with the majority of the spiderlings sitting on her back. As Rosie and Baba watched, the rest began to rapidly clamber up her legs to join their siblings.

"There you go, Rosie," said Baba. "She give perfect birth. Nothing to worry about. She just find somewhere safe because upset by moving. Now baby stay mostly on her back for next few week. They get free ride."

As they watched, a baby trying to squirm up Divana's leg got knocked back, once, then twice. He tumbled and landed upside down on the egg with the web design, then slid down the side, legs waving wildly. He rocked on his tiny round back, righted himself, hopped up the side of the egg and launched himself fiercely at his mom's leg.

He climbed determinedly until he was on the very top of the heap of babies on her back. The little guy triumphantly waved a leg back and forth. "He looks like a conductor signaling the orchestra," said Rosie.

"He think he the boss," said Baba.

The spiderling balanced himself on four of his siblings and began serious spider push ups. Up down up down, rock from side to side. Up down up down, rock from side to side.

"He's hilarious," said Rosie. "He's just like his Mom. I definitely want to keep that one."

"Good idea, Rosie," Baba replied. "I like how he not give up when he have big problem. He would make good immigrant. Come on, let's take basket of pysanky into your room so spider stay in there. Your mother feel little bit crazy over this. She love those tiny chicken so much, soon she bring in house. They would love baby spider for snack. You understand my meaning?"

"Yes," said Rosie. She made a mental note that the clownish baby had a unique pale dot on the back of his head, so she could find him again. "But doesn't Mom understand that killing Divana's babies would kill our good luck?"

"Is just story to her, Rosie. Good one, but just story." Baba carefully picked up the basket. Rosie ran ahead and cleared ornaments off her bookshelf, so Divana could be near the window.

Rosie turned the light on by her bookshelf, and she and Baba took one last good look at the new family. "I wonder how the spiderlings cling to Divana's back," Rosie wondered.

"They not so good rider as you, Rosie," Baba replied. "They hang on to little knobby hair on Divana's back. That like you hanging on saddle horn. But it work for them. Goodnight, poopchik. We talk more tomorrow." She yawned and then plodded wearily down the hall.

With her mind full of images of baby spiders riding horses on the spiral web, Rosie drifted off to sleep.

The next day, Rosie slept in. She awoke to see Divana exploring the new closet, with her entire litter of spiderlings riding on her back.

"No web, Divana?" asked Rosie, then answered her own question. "Oh, of course not. Your little squirmies would get stuck in it. You're welcome to live on the pysanky or make a nest in the closet, if you like."

Baba knocked on Rosie's door shortly after eleven a.m. "Come in," said Rosie. Divana was resting on the floor at the foot of Rosie's bed. "Your Mom and Dad take care of feed and clean horse this morning," said Baba.

"That was nice of them," said Rosie. "It was still my turn."

She related the dream she'd had about Divana singing to her babies. "You sure it was dream?" asked Baba. "It sound real to me."

She squinted at Divana and the babies. "Look like three hundred...", her mouth moved soundlessly. "Fifty seven," she said, and clucked her tongue. She kissed Rosie on the forehead. "Come in to kitchen, I make *kobasa* and egg," she said.

"Okay," said Rosie as she picked up pencil and paper. "But first I'm going to write down Divana's new lyrics. I think they'd make a cool rock song. Baba?"

"Yes?"

"What's Mom going to do when we tell her there are three hundred and fifty seven babies?"

"She going to freak out. We handle it." Baba's brown eyes widened enormously. The heavy fringe of black lashes sprang in all directions. "Just remember, keep bedroom door closed, and listen for sound of small chicken feet in house."

"Whoa. That's *ominous*," said Rosie.

She picked up a pen and quickly scribbled what she remembered from the night before. Then she followed the scent of fried garlic sausage, putting thoughts of spiders aside.

CHAPTER THIRTEEN

The housewarming party was a week after the move. Rosie had monopolized the phone so frequently, her parents said she'd have to buy her own. The family decided to also make it an early thirteenth birthday party for Rosie, so her friends could enjoy the farm before the gloomy BC fall rains.

One by one, Rosie's friends arrived at the door, each carrying a present and some with baseball gloves. Brad handed Rosie a small, clean artichoke jar full of flies for Divana. Michie's parents helped her carry a large, mysterious object into the house. Christopher and Leanne came from across the road. Rosie had invited her friends to bring their grandmothers for their own party in the living room and kitchen.

Mom was away at a weekend retreat for people with eating disorders, *Dying to be Perfect*. Dad had taken a room on the retreat grounds to support her.

The kitchen was redolent with the delicious smell of borshch, which Baba and Rosie had cooked the day before. Mom's specialty, crab apple pie, sat at the centre of the table. She hadn't tasted even a forkful. Stefan's Baba arrived carrying a bowl of buttered *varenyky,* or perogies. She was hourglass-shaped and stylishly dressed in a green raw silk skirt suit. Micheline's grandmere was tall and solid, and brought with her a fragrant tourtiere. She was in a plain, dove gray dress of scratchy-looking fabric. Peggy's nana carried a casserole dish of Irish stew.

Aleisha's grandmother was round and smiley with

dimpled cheeks. She'd brought a casserole dish of jambalaya. Her hair was done up in a braid that went all the way around her head, and she wore a long, colourful skirt.

Baba wore her best cardigan. Which was red and buttoned on only two buttons, just like her every day one. "Why mess with good thing?" she replied when Rosie tried to persuade to wear a different colour.

"I hear you have a lucky spider in the house," said Aleisha's grandmother. "Aleisha came home with the Baba spider song, and I just love it. I'd like to tell you about Anansi, the African trickster spider. I think we have some other things in common, as well."

Baba grinned and patted the chair between her and Stefan's baba. "We gonna be good friend," she replied. "Now have something to eat."

Rosie welcomed her guests into the den, which she had decorated with blue crepe paper streamers and multi-coloured balloons. She had on a CD of her favorite songs. After they'd put down their gifts and taken a quick look around the house, Rosie led them to the pasture. Jessie and Billie were grazing at the far end, but came trotting to the fence when Rosie called. She gave each of her friends a carrot. "Make sure you let go before they get to the end, you guys. Fingers look an awful lot like carrots."

Michie stroked and fed Jessie and Billie with an ecstatic look on her face. She turned to Rosie with shining eyes. "I'm getting riding lessons soon, Rosie," she said. "I can hardly wait."

Rosie felt a leap of joy inside as she briefly imagined the two of them riding side by side. She squashed it. *Michie will be as wimpy on a horse as she is about everything else.*

Jessie and Billie stood patiently for everyone's petting until they realized they'd seen the last of the goodies. They turned back to the serious business of grazing, tails swishing contentedly.

After a look around the barn, where they admired the softly gleaming saddles and bridles, the group headed to the back yard.

As Peggy's family had gone on a road trip at the end of June, this was her first time at the farm. When she saw Peep and Beep, she dropped to her knees to look more closely and said, "What sweetie pies! Rosie, where can I get mini chickens?"

"Good news," Rosie replied. "Peep has been laying an egg now and then. If you want a couple of babies, I bet my mom will let them hatch."

Rosie was thrilled to have a yard large enough for at least a limited game of scrub baseball. Dad had poured sand into burlap feed sacks for bases, and the windowless barn wall served as a backstop.

"Look," Rosie said as the group organized themselves. "A baseball diamond is like a web, with the players running along the strands. Which reminds me. I'd like to show you guys Divana's babies later."

Michie shuddered.

Rosie turned her back. *Get over it, princess. I'm tired of being the gutsy one.* A cramped and rotten corner of the web inside her floated free. As the short strands slid apart, a bitter taste rose in her throat.

They played ball until each person had had two turns at bat, then voted to quit and wash up for dinner.

Back in the house, the sweaty group flopped down on the couch and floor. Rosie picked up an empty juice pitcher and a couple of crushed plastic cups. She headed down the hallway to the kitchen. She heard Micheline's name, and stopped outside the door.

"You know," said Micheline's rather stern grandmere in a French accent, "Michie is so upset that she and Rosie fought. She is not the kind of girl to show even Rosie this, but she has cried over it many times."

"Rosie upset too," Baba replied, picking at some pie crumbs. "They been friends long time."

"I tell her this over and over, that spider can be good luck. But you know, when person have fear in here," Grandmere tapped her stomach, "This can be *tres difficile* to change. I tell her spider is good luck because it tell us what to expect. In French, we say, 'Araignée du matin—chagrin; Araignée du midi—plaisir; Araignée du soir—espoir.'"

"Mmmm. That sounds beautiful," said Aleisha's grandma, who had closed her eyes as if to hear better.

Micheline's grandmere translated, "'A spider seen in the morning is a sign of grief; a spider seen at noon, of joy; a spider seen in the evening, of hope.' Michie know this in her head, but her body is terrify of spider. 'I can't, I can't,' she say to me. 'I love Rosie with all my heart, but I can't.'"

"What you do when she so scared?" asked Baba.

Grandmere let out a long, noisy sigh. "I discuss with her, of course. But you know, confidence has been what they call 'issue' since my son adopt her. She hurt pretty bad by birth family until she was four year old. We all get counsel, but still..."

The other grandmothers clucked sympathetically.

Rosie stood silently for a moment, swaying. She braced her right hand on the wall. *I didn't know.*

Baba put her hand on grandmere's. "I never tell Rosie how Michie hurt when she baby," she said. "She know her friend adopted, but we wait for Michie to tell her whole story. Worst thing is for Rosie to feel sorry, like her best friend have some kind defect."

Rosie dropped into a crouch and cradled her head on her knees, still clutching the plastic cups. She had to expand her ribs at the back in order to breathe. She raised her head; the hallway expanded and contracted in wavy lines. *I've been acting as if she's defective because she's not like me.*

"Why Michie not tell Rosie yet?" Stefan's baba sounded puzzled. She reached over to the bowl of perogies and picked out one that had come undone. Soft cheese crumbs spilled from its edges. She stood up and placed it on a plate by the sink.

"She's ashamed," said Aleisha's grandma, putting down her spoonful of borshch. "I learned that from the grandchildren of slaves in Louisiana, including myself. People who've been abused somehow feel it's their fault. Even when they were powerless in the situation. Sometimes I feel ashamed we were homeless after Hurricane Katrina."

"I heard that about my great-grandparents during the Irish potato famine," said Peggy's nana, shaking her head.

Baba clenched her fists. "I still have dream I fighting against Soviet and Nazi. I feel terrible shame I let them win," she said. Aleisha's grandma looked at her tenderly.

"Yes, Michie never going to have kind of confidence like Rosie," grandmere said as she poured a ladle of jambalaya over sweet rice. "She always going to feel like she maybe not completely belong. Even if just in small way. Is not about spider. She is not confident about way she look, about way she dance, all sorts of things. And when she feel bad about herself, then she can say some very mean things to people."

"She perfect way she is," said Baba firmly, planting her fork in some tourtiere as if she were preparing to raise a flag. "Is important to treat her that way. She tell Rosie whole story when she good and ready. Person need to feel strong inside before they can show they weak."

Rosie put down the cups and slumped against the wall. *I've been acting like I'm the only one who's hurt. Help.* She breathed deeply and looked inside. She found the swirling but firmly anchored place where her core was attached to the universe, and silently called on the golden rain of medicine. After a few moments, a warm wave of bliss washed over her. She stood up, still a bit shaky, and stepped on a plastic cup. Crunch.

Stefan's baba called, "Come in here and get food, little ones."

Rosie and her friends feasted on the wonderful array of foods. Rosie had trouble getting her meal down, but she tried each dish and made polite comments to the grandmothers.

Dessert was crab apple pie and ice cream. Rosie didn't want a cake until her *real* birthday. She figured blowing out the candles on the wrong day was bad luck.

Presents were another matter. She tore into the colourful gift wrapping paper. Christopher and Leanne leaned forward eagerly as Rosie unwrapped a brand new, royal blue halter. "We noticed Jessie's was faded, and she's way too pretty for that," said Leanne. "We're glad you're our new neighbour, Rosie. We're going to have great times riding together."

Rosie glanced at Michie, who swallowed hard. *It must be horrible to think about almost losing my friendship, and now she sees me making horse buddies.*

There was a paperback of folk tales from Peggy and *Prismacolor* pencils from Mark. Aleisha had brought a package of apple-flavoured horse treats, wrapped in a soft flannel cloth. "I think it's hilarious that your coach told you to polish your horse," she explained. "I thought you might need some new cloth."

"What, no mean gumbo for Jessie?" asked Rosie.

"Nah. She's gotta work up to being a New Orleans horse," Aleisha replied.

Rosie exclaimed over each present. For a moment, she imagined Barb and Shelley filling two seats in the den. The Protection Dial in her chest glowed and gave a chirp, then faded. She shook off the vision.

Stefan had kept his gift by his side, and handed it to Rosie with his face flaming. It was a body brush with *Rosie* burned into the wooden back. "Your new horses deserve a new brush. I wrote the inscription in woodworking class."

Rosie felt an itch in her legs. She jumped up and put her newest Kesha CD in the player, then opened Brad's gift, a little brass plate engraved with her name. He briefly narrowed his eyes at Stefan, then said, "You fasten that to the back of your saddle. The lady at the tack store said all the girls in Pony Club have them."

Micheline's gift was by the door. Rosie had saved it for last, and now moved quickly to open it. It was a four foot tall rectangle, covered in iridescent silver paper. Micheline said, "Be careful, it's fragile."

Rosie pulled a small section of paper away from the

mysterious shape within. A long, deep green leaf sprang out. Further unwrapping revealed a thin cardboard casing that protected a huge, luxurious tropical plant striped in vivid red, turquoise and yellow. "Oh Michie, it's amazing. It looks like a parrot!" said Rosie.

"My parents drove me to two different nurseries to find something like that. I thought Divana and her babies would enjoy climbing on it," Micheline replied. "They can use it as a sort of spider playground. You'll have to put bugs on it yourself, though." She smiled weakly.

"That's so great of you, Michie," said Rosie, and gave her a hug. "It's perfect for them to learn how to hunt like wolves." She looked carefully at Micheline's face, which had turned faintly green. "I know how hard it must have been to think of something like this. Thank you."

After everyone had had a chance to admire her gifts, Rosie said, "I'd like you all to see Divana's babies. We'll go in my room just two at a time, so you don't scare them."

"Wicked! Great! Sweet! " said the three boys.

Micheline took a few deep breaths. Since The Spider Incident, she'd only hung out in Rosie's living room and yard, and that just occasionally.

"I'd like to try," said Michie quietly. She stood up and took a step.

"You only have to go as far as you can. I don't mind," Rosie replied.

Michie gulped. "Why don't we carry in the plant together?" she suggested. She and Rosie picked it up and placed it just inside the bedroom doorway, Michie blocking her own view by keeping her face behind the leafiest part.

Divana was sitting on Rosie's bookcase, half obscuring the title of *Old Yeller*. Most of the spiderlings clung to her back, while a few brave souls trundled around her legs. "Okay, Rosie, I'm going to go veeeerrrry sllllllooooooowwly," said Michie. She creeped out from behind the plant, hand clutched to her stomach. Rosie reached out and took her hand. They made it halfway to the bookcase with Rosie leading. Then Micheline leaned forward a little. She came a few steps closer to be side by side with Rosie. "Oh my goodness," she said.

The clownish baby was in his favorite place, balanced on top of the others. He leaped once, all eight legs spread eagle in the air, and landed solidly. Rosie watched Michie's face anxiously. She peered intently at the little guy. As if he knew he needed to put on his best show, he spun around, then began a series of push ups. When another baby shifted beneath him, he balanced on the next. Then he did something new. He balanced on four legs, then two, his round rump in the air as far as it could go. Micheline burst out laughing.

"That's the funniest thing I've ever seen!" she said. "Rosie, he is so cuuuuute!"

Rosie was astonished. "Do you really like him?"

"Oh yeah. I'm scared of adult spiders, but how can you not love this guy?" The grin on her face was genuine. "And the rest of them look like Gummi Bears. They're not scary at all. But poor Divana, having to carry them all."

"That guy is my favorite, too," Rosie replied. She wrinkled her forehead. "Michie, would you like to have him?"

"You're kidding."

"No, I'm not. I'd like to give him to you as a present." She quickly rummaged through her closet and found the Chinese take out box. She waved it by its wire handle. The symbol for luck glinted. "He'll be ready to leave his mom in about three weeks, and you can take him home in this."

"I'd love that, Rosie, thank you." Michie turned the box in her hands. "How will you know when he's ready to leave?" she asked.

"When the babies stop riding on Divana's back and they're using your jungle gym to catch insects," Rosie replied, grinning.

Micheline cocked her head and looked more closely at Divana. "Thank you for bringing him into the world, Mother Spider," she whispered. "You're not as ugly as I thought." She turned to Rosie, her eyes sparkling. "Grandmere told me a spider seen in the afternoon brings joy. I think she's right."

Divana waved a leg, but both girls had turned away. They went back into the living room, where their friends were already dancing.

CHAPTER FOURTEEN

"She can't even look at that empty stall, Michie," Rosie said. "When she sees me on Jessie, she turns her head away to hide the tears."

The two girls were on a dirt lane behind the farm, practicing bike acrobatics. They were both rusty, but Michie had finally sustained one wheelie after a jump, with the goal of three in a row.

Baba had been accompanying Rosie to the barn for most morning and evening feedings, and her longing was apparent.

"Why doesn't she come out with it and say she wants her own horse?" asked Michie. "She's pretty darn direct the rest of the time." Michie was wearing a chocolate brown pair of riding breeches. She'd worn them all week in anticipation of her first lesson.

"She knows how tight money is, and she's pretending to *love* just hanging out with the horses. She's been coaching me to stand up on Jessie's back while she rides Billie, but you can tell she thinks of him as Dad's horse," Rosie replied, tucking her hair under her helmet with annoyed jabs.

"My riding coach said a horse like Baba's Misha would cost thousands of dollars in Canada. Ukrainians were the first people to tame horses, so we had the best ones until the Soviets stole and slaughtered them. I'm keeping the water bucket in that stall full, anyway."

"Isn't there, like, a horse Humane Society?" Michie asked. "Maybe she can adopt one for cheap. I mean, look how great

Jessie turned out, even after being abused as a baby."

Rosie's mouth fell open. "She sure did. She's the *greatest*. Race you to the computer, Michie," she said.

The girls galloped down the road shoulder to shoulder. Rosie's streaked gold and Michie's glossy dark mane mingled inside a cloud of dust.

Back home, the girls snuck the family photo albums into Rosie's room. They found just the picture they needed.

Three weeks later, after the horses and chickens had been fed and turned out, the family gathered by the car. Mom and Dad placed a big picnic basket in the trunk.

"Where we going, people?" Baba asked.

Rosie answered, "It's a surprise, and that's all I'm going to say." She made a zippering motion across her mouth.

Michie stepped out of her Dad's Jeep just as Mom glanced at her watch with a frown. "Sorry I'm late folks!" she said. She and Rosie briefly linked pinkies as they got in the back seat.

It was a long drive. They passed small towns on their way east. Rosie and Michie challenged each other to spot Volkswagens, then red cars, and finally bet an ice cream cone on who would be the first to see a llama. Michie spied an alpaca, and for the next twenty minutes, the girls argued over whether it was or was not the same thing. Baba snoozed, mouth hanging open.

The girls were still bickering when Dad pulled over at a roadside ice cream stand. Baba awoke with a snarfling sound. "Your banyak argument make turn my stomach," she said grumpily. "It completely pointless. Give me all kind nightmare."

The vendor scooped hard ice cream into cones, and the debate was forgotten in the excitement of choosing from the old fashioned flavours. Rosie picked rainbow, Michie chocolate, Dad tiger stripe, Mom strawberry (her first in two years), and Baba vanilla with sprinkles. Rosie and Michie chewed their sugar cones right down, then sucked the last of the melted ice cream from the pointed bottoms.

As soon as they pulled away from the stand, the llama/alpaca conflict restarted. Dad said, "Hey, I thought this thing was resolved when Mom and I paid for *both* your cones."

"Apparently, you were wrong," said Mom drily, wiping a bit of pink ice cream from her blouse. "The girls' mouths were just full."

"Alpacas are miniature llamas," said Micheline with her jaw set. "They're related, the same way as ponies are to horses."

Rosie crossed her arms. "Oh, they are not! It's a completely different *species*."

"I am so tired your arguing," said Baba. "They close enough related species, smarty pants Rosie. They can have marriage and baby together. Michie win for once. Now be quiet before you make my head split."

Rosie and Michie sat silently for the next twenty minutes. Once Baba dozed off again, Michie whispered, "Greasy species, you make my head split."

Rosie whispered back, "You make turn my stomach, smarty pants girl." A smile started in the corner of her mouth.

Michie giggled. "I'll bet you *two* ice cream cones you can't spot a llama and alpaca getting married," she said. "You're on," Rosie replied. The girls gave each other one good pinch on the arm each, and peace returned to the back seat.

An half hour later, Dad turned the old Buick into a driveway with a sign that had a horse head burned into it. "We getting more horse?" asked Baba.

"Just one," Rosie replied. She leaned against Baba, and felt the old woman's heart thumping hard.

A pack of dogs galloped to meet the car. There was a German Shepherd with strong black markings on his silver coat, a red Doberman bitch with lovely floppy ears, and two small, smooth coated terrier-looking dogs of indeterminate mix. They barked furiously and wagged their tails at the same time. A middle-aged man with a kindly face walked across the farmyard towards them.

"They're friends!" he said to the dogs, and they quieted immediately, settling themselves around his legs. "I'm Mr. Prockert. You must be here about the big mare," he said to the family through the open windows. Rosie gave a quick nod and Dad winked.

A group of foals gazed curiously at them through the fence, their dams grazing behind, now and then watchfully raising their heads. "Where we are?" asked Baba.

"This is a rescue facility for horses," Mr. Prockert answered. "We take in ones that have been abused or neglected, restore them to health and them find adopters for them."

There was a loud bray from behind them. He smiled and said, "On the way, we've picked up a few other animals."

He gestured towards the pasture, where three goats and a shaggy Sicilian donkey had joined the horses in peering at the visitors. "Maaaaaaaah," said a white goat with curly horns. "Baaaaah, maaaaah," added a chocolate brown and a tri-coloured. A buckskin foal leaped in the air and added a treble whinny to the chorus.

"They're all so cute!" said Rosie, "Maybe one day our farm will have this many animals."

Mom and Dad looked at each other. Baba beamed. "From your mouth to God's ear, Rosie," she said. "This what being rich look like."

"Absolutely right," Mr. Prockert replied. "All our money goes towards looking after the animals, but we're rich in love. We get a fair number that are voluntarily surrendered by their owners, and rescues from PMU farms. "Shall we?" he gestured towards the barn.

Baba had trouble getting out of the car. It looked as if her legs weren't working so well, but she refused Dad's arm. "Day I can't walk to horse, is day I die," she grumped.

Mr. Prockert led them towards a paddock at the side of the barn. Baba sped up so that by the time they got to the corner, she was at the front of the group, swollen ankles and shaky knees be darned. She turned the corner and gasped.

She was face to face with a large, solid mare, white as snow with soft dark eyes. The mare snorted and bobbed her head, her delicate nostrils reaching towards Baba's scent.

Baba took the magnificent face between her hands and blew softly in the mare's nose. The animal breathed back. A shiver went up Rosie's spine.

"Would you like to try her?" asked Mr. Prockert. "She's wonderful under saddle. She was starved and beaten by some terrible people, so she's wary of most. But she's healthy now, and myself and the volunteers where she came from have spent a great deal of time with her. I think with the right person she'll be just perfect."

Baba kept her face along the mare's smooth cheek, trying to hide that tears were flowing freely along her own wrinkled ones. "Yes, she already tell me she fall in hand of fascist." Her fingers traced a rope scar on the mare's graceful neck. "I tell Misha they not steal her away again. I kill them first, not wait for spider. Was my fault, last time I lose courage. Is time to ride again."

A deep rumble resonated in the mare's chest, the kind of sound that comforts a foal.

"Mama, it *wasn't* your fault," Dad said urgently. "Men came to the village with guns and tanks..." He was shaking.

Mom put a hand on his arm. "Shhhhh," she said, "Let her work it through. Feelings aren't logical." She took Dad's hand and squeezed it. "And you went through plenty of grief and hardship in Ukraine yourself, honey. It's okay to get upset about it," she said.

"No, it wasn't Baba's fault," said Rosie under her breath. "It's never the abused person's fault."

"I'll get a saddle, then," Mr. Prockert said.

Rosie had found the rescue facility on the Internet. She told the kind man exactly what kind of horse they were looking for, and what had happened to Baba's Misha. He said he was more than pleased for the opportunity to heal both a traumatized horse and an old woman's pain.

He interviewed her coach and Mrs. McIvor about Rosie's

family, then sent word through his Canadian and American network of horse rescuers. One group passing on word to the next, they located a horse true to Rosie's detailed description from a family photograph and Baba's reminiscences.

Everyone agreed Baba would be getting a quality horse who looked much like Misha.

The family left Baba talking to the white mare, and retreated to the car. Rosie pulled out a shopping bag that contained Baba's riding pants and a pair of boots.

"I knew we gave them an accurate description of Mama's horse, but who could have predicted their instant affinity for each other?" said Dad, his face glowing.

"It's like magic," said Michie.

"The web is spinning," said Rosie quietly. "It's the golden medicine I saw pouring down on us when we were blessing Divana. Some of it fell on Baba and Misha. That mare has Misha's soul."

Rosie was startled at the strange words that flowed from her mouth, from a source with which she wasn't familiar. And yet a deep resonance through her middle let her know she was speaking the truth, the truth of the spiral web.

She felt compelled to continue, "She knew how badly Baba needs her, and she came back. I wonder why Misha had to go through being abused, though. It doesn't seem fair."

"No, it's not fair, Rosie," Dad answered. "But your baba went through horrific times in Ukraine, too. She lost everything and many people she held dear. Think of how hers and Misha's love for each other will be even deeper this time around."

"No, it isn't fair,Rosie," said Michie, "But think about how *our* friendship is even better after we had a fight. We understand each other more. Hard times can have happy endings." The girls stood awkwardly for a moment.

"I think so," Rosie replied. "Then you guys believe what I said about that mare really being Misha?" She looked up from beneath her brows.

"Oh yeah," said Michie. "That's obvious. I was surprised,

that's all. But I shouldn't be.

Dad nodded. "Life would be unbearable if loved ones were lost to us forever. The One who created the universe lets some awful things happen, but She couldn't be that relentlessly cruel," he said.

"Is that part of 'energy can neither be created nor destroyed?'" asked Rosie.

"Um," replied Mom. "Technically speaking..."

Rosie interrupted her. "I've been reading Mrs. Einstein's old letters with Baba. Physics is our passion, next to horses. Baba says the value of science is to make Ukrainian legends clearer, and to help people live their lives better."

"You're over my head again," said Michie.

They heard voices by the paddock. Mr. Prockert was saddling the white mare. Mom walked over with Baba's gear, and the man pointed the two of them towards the barn washroom. In a few minutes, Baba emerged wearing formfitting black stretch breeches. Mr. Prockert led the mare into the riding ring, and gave Baba a boost up while Dad head the mare's head. With one hoarse "Oi!" she was in the saddle.

"Oy yoi *yoi*," she said grumpily, "When I young woman, I jump on tall horse bareback. Stupid arthritis make me stiff," she said as she settled her large, round body in the saddle and gathered the reins. The mare was over sixteen solid hands, easily able to support her.

As the family watched, Baba transformed. The body whose softness they took comfort in hugging and cuddling straightened to nearly military posture. Her wrinkled hands gripped the reins firmly, strong calf muscles clasped the horse's ribs, and her eyes became sharply focused. Misha collected herself, neck arched and weight balanced on her hindquarters. Baba moved the mare briskly forward.

To Rosie's delight, they were soon cantering gracefully around the large paddock, the reins in lightest contact with the mare's mouth. Baba guided Misha in precise circles and figure eights. "You look gorgeous, Baba!" Rosie called.

A number of the pastured horses, donkeys and goats had wandered over to the adjoining fence and were softly nickering, braying and bleating agreement. The chocolate brown goat had his head pressed firmly against the wire mesh between the bottom two fence slats, and was following every stride with large golden eyes.

Michie gripped Rosie's arm. "Your Baba wasn't just telling stories about her horsemanship," she said. "She rides like a goddess." Baba guided her Misha over a low jump, the two of them in perfect balance. The mare's coat gleamed silver in the noonday sun, and she moved as if she were floating.

"Oh yeah," said Rosie, smiling at Michie. "It only sounds like she makes things up. That's part of the beauty. She tells true lies, like all good storytellers."

Rosie put her hands on her belly, breathed deeply and looked into her own future. She would be as fine a horsewoman as Baba, she would earn her place on the spiral web of horsewomen throughout history. She would never listen to anyone telling her she was too old or too fat or too this or too that to take pleasure in her body and the ways she could use it. And she would be a deeply beloved storyteller, too.

Rosie turned back to Michie. "That's the female power that Baba talks about," she said, leaning on the board fence. "It comes down the centre of her body, into the horse's, and back to her again. No matter what the mare does, Baba never shifts from centre. Even with everything that happened to her, she held on to that part of herself. "

"Yeah," Michie replied, "I've felt a bit of that when we're jumping our bikes. I guess by the time you're old, it's totally awesome."

"Wait till you have some riding lessons, Michie," said Rosie. "That's when I really started getting it."

Baba was puffing and perspiring after her ride. Mr. Prockert and Dad helped her dismount. "Maybe I go to aerobic with Mom after all," she said to Dad. "And you need build me mounting block for home. Horse is mine, right?"

she asked in a quavering voice. "Good horse like this, she worth many thousand dollar."

"Oh yes, Mama, she's yours," Dad replied. "Don't worry about the money."

"Not at all," said Mr. Prockert. "This is one of the horses in our care who has a sponsor in the community. You can just make a small donation to our rescue organization, and trailer her home this week. It brings me a great deal of pleasure to see you and the mare hit it off. She was a tough case, wouldn't let me lay a hand on her for a week. I have to say, I've never seen a horse and horsewoman more suited to each other. "

"It's as if all the donations we've made to rescues for years, suddenly came back to us in good luck," said Rosie.

"I never would have said this a couple of months ago, but I think your taking Divana in brought good luck," said Michie.

Mom's face spasmed. Rosie's stomach flipped.

Baba took Rosie's hand. "World is magic place, Rosie," she said. "Giving home to Divana and babies please the Great Mother. Make us part of creation."

"I was never good at physics, Rosie," Dad added, "But I can tell you this: all the love we'll ever need has been created, and love cannot be destroyed. It just keeps coming back in different forms. Misha was meant to be with Baba."

"Just like we were meant to be friends forever,"Rosie said to Michie.

"That sounds right," Michie replied.

A long, plaintive "Maaaaaaaaa!" sounded behind them.

Mr. Prockert cleared his throat. "As I told you on the phone," he said to Mom, "There's one condition for taking the white mare."

"Always is condition," Baba said, crossing her arms and squinting. "First is big flattery, then condition. Just like in Soviet Union. They tell us we have wonderful thing with Communism. Instead, they take everything away."

Mr. Prockert put his hand on her arm and said, "No, no, don't worry. Let me show you what I mean."

113

The man walked over to the gate separating pasture and paddock and opened it. The brown goat trotted stiffly to Misha, his long black ears flopping with each stride. The mare bowed her neck and nuzzled him, nipping gently along the ridge of hair on his spine. He stretched his neck in a "U" shape to comical, rubbery thinness and licked her chin.

"The mare has a companion animal to steady her nerves. They sleep together," Mr. P said. "He came with her as a rescue at the same time. They're inseparable."

Rosie said softly, "Perfect." The Protection Dial in her heart swung freely to *Wide Open*, then glowed and hummed somewhere off the meter. She took Micheline's hand.

"The mare was wearing holes in the floor of her stall, walking all night, until they got together. He'd been treated as miserably as her, and they comforted each other before either of them would come near people. She wouldn't even buddy up with other horses at first. He has to go home with the mare." Mr. P scratched the goat's ear. "This is Sunny, short for Sunshine. She's *his* family."

"I think he very dear goat," said Baba. "I know what mean not to sleep, so miserable," she added, putting her hands on Misha and Sunny. The goat leaned into her and grunted.

"Me too," said Michie.

"Me three," said Rosie. "Hey, I wonder if Sunny has a bathing suit?" She grinned at Baba. "We'll have to be careful about his ears in the jacuzzi, though."

"Maybe you could set the pump on low," Michie suggested.

Mr. P's eyebrows rocketed upwards. "What..." he began.

"Never mind," said Baba, lifting her chin. "They have very strange sense humour. Get from crazy parents, always make fun of serious thing."

"Hey," said Rosie to Mr. P, "Do you like spiders? We have a bunch that need homes."

CHAPTER FIFTEEN

Misha stepped from the trailer like the queen she was, silvery head high and nostrils flaring. Jessie and Billie galloped to the pasture fence and whinnied, long trumpet blasts of curiosity and welcome. Sunny emerged at the top of the ramp and surveyed the farmyard, his head weaving this way and that at the end of his flexible neck. One golden eye fixed on the red chickens, and he trotted towards them.

Baba proudly led the gleaming mare into a paddock next to the pasture, so the three horses could get acquainted without kicking each other.

And like the queen *she* was, Divana presided over her babies, one hundred and fifty of whom were busy using Micheline's exotic plant as a spider gym. The clownish guy was among the advanced group, busily running and hopping up and down the multi-coloured leaves. The other two hundred and seven still clung to Divana's back.

Rosie sat on the bed, sketching her new family and thinking about how to distribute three hundred and fifty seven spiders. Mom poked her head in the door and grimaced at the spiderlings. "Soon, Rosie," she said, narrowing her eyes. "Or I'll take care of the matter myself."

"You don't *understand*, Mom," said Rosie, jabbing her pencil into the paper. "I need to know what Baba Spider means for me to do with Divana's babies."

Mom made a gagging sound. "You are entirely too fanciful. Sometimes I can't believe you're *my* daughter." She slapped the wall before striding off.

Rosie looked after her for a moment, the corners of her mouth drawn down. She drew circles and squiggles, spiders one at a time and in groups. Her mind was squirming. She felt like jumping out of her skin.

She drew a stick figure with wire rim glasses in a ballet tutu, then wrapped her fist around the pencil and slashed dark lines over it. She pulled on her riding boots and went outside. Over the paddock fence, the black and red horses were taking turns touching noses with the big white newcomer, each blowing and occasionally letting out a sharp squeal.

Baba was leaning on the paddock fence watching. The rest of the family had decided to avoid added stress to Misha by leaving them alone. Sunny lay in a corner munching hay with Peep and Beep roosting on his back. They had fluffed up so they looked twice their usual size, their beaks teeny orange triangles almost lost in the red feathers.

"Hi Baba, how's it going?" Rosie asked.

"Oy, they make big fuss at first, but calming down now. Next day or two, Misha go in pasture with them."

"Do you think it would be okay if I took Jessie out now?"

"Probably be good. Then Misha and Billie make friend, no jealousy."

"We're going to ride together real soon, Baba."

Rosie led Jessie in, groomed and saddled her. She caught her breath each time she was near the mare, whose blend of delicate angles and powerful contours made her as striking as any story book horse. She was a breathing bronze sculpture clothed in black velvet. Better than any fantasy could possibly be, Jessie was *real*. And Baba was right, her rough beginning added depth to her personality.

Rosie's long hair was in a classic French braid, neatly pinned up. Aleisha had shown her some styling tricks, and, in return, could now draw pretty good animals.

Rosie set out for the trails that surrounded her new community. For the first few minutes, Jessie occasionally swung her head back, drew a deep breath that stretched her ribcage hugely, and nickered at the horses left behind. But she kept moving smoothly forward, light and obedient to Rosie's legs and hands.

Rosie concentrated on the strange feeling in her belly, and Baba's words about finding and staying in the centre. *The centre, the centre. What do I know about the baby spiders if I pay attention to my centre?*

As she turned Jessie onto the main trail, she realized it circled the entire community, and branches led to each farm and the woods from it. She was riding an immense web. This web was inside the endless one that formed the universe. Rosie felt her seat sink deeply into the centre of Jessie's body.

Wherever I am, is centre. I can ride all around this trail, or down any of the branches, and I'm still at the centre. Because it's in me. It's in Jessie, too. And Baba, and Mom, and Dad, and Michie. And we're in the centre of Baba Spider's web, at the same time. Just like Divana brought luck to both her spiderlings and the humans who rescued her, it makes no difference to the Creator whether creatures are human, horse or spider. Our futures are woven together. We're equally important.

A vision formed in her mind. She saw a way to find homes for the baby spiderlings, where they could bring good luck in the future, woven with a plan to help animals that needed someone to love them as fiercely as she loved Jessie.

Now I know how Divana feels just before she lets the silk flow from her body to spin a web. I know the special thing I'm meant to do with her babies. They came to me for a reason. Good luck doesn't just come from her. I'm part of making good luck, with my actions. Thank you, Baba Spider.

Rosie nudged Jessie into a trot, and they explored several

trails. Her excitement grew, and she asked for a canter. They wove in and out of intersecting branches until the horse was lightly sweating and Rosie's legs were sore. By the time they were ready to walk home, she had a plan. Several times on the way back to the barn, Jessie turned her large kind eye towards Rosie.

Rosie and Baba led in the horses for their evening feed. A lump surfaced in Rosie's throat as she watched Baba lead Misha into the long-empty stall. While Baba was unbuckling her halter, the big white mare briefly pressed her head against the old woman's chest. She, too, had journeyed to a strange country and found refuge from horror.

Over a dinner of *holubtsi*, Rosie said, "Here's the first part of my plan. We need to give as many people in our community baby spiders as we can. It's our blessing to them, just like when we blessed Divana before she gave birth." She briefly described her vision of the spirals.

"You really getting it, Rosie," said Baba, gesturing with her fork.

Rosie took another juicy cabbage roll. Mom said, "Look how much you've already eaten..." then clamped her mouth shut.

Dad ran his fingers along the tablecloth's flower embroidery. "Rosie, most people won't understand what you mean about being 'blessed by spiders'. Remember how Michie reacted?"

"No *kidding*," said Mom.

Baba replied, "There always way around. We make kind of ceremony, so everyone feel they doing something special. One thing I miss about Ukraina is way whole village get together for special occasion."

"Listen. That's the other part of my idea. I've been thinking about all the animals we've rescued in the past while," said Rosie. "A frozen spider and over three hundred babies, a beat up horse and a lonely goat. Jessie is my dream come true. But I feel like *we're* the ones who've been rescued by the animals. Look at what they've added to our lives."

She spun the Lazy Susan and reached for the salad. "I have a plan for how we can help a bunch of abused animals find homes at the same time." She laid it out between bites of plump tomato and home grown butter lettuce.

"I don't know," said Mom. "It sounds far-fetched. I can't see how you'd make it work. Be realistic, Rosie."

"To rescue animal is far-fetched like me and your husband escaping Soviet Union," said Baba quietly. "Abused animal is kind of immigrant, too. If Canada not rescue us, we maybe already be dead from no doctor and too much hard work. My sister, she die just from broken leg. Person have to try."

"Not the same thing," said Mom.

Rosie's frustration with Mom and the tenderness she felt towards suffering creatures had been blending into a powerful brew. The vegetables in her mouth tasted filthy, electric. She shifted a large piece of tomato into her cheek. She was suddenly a berserk volcano, a wild thunderstorm, a mad Midwest tornado.

She exploded in furious tears. "Is there anything else you don't want me to do, mother? You don't want me to get dirty or protect Divana's babies or help abused animals find homes. You want a sweet skinny daughter who plays with dolls and wears lace dresses, not a loud fat lump like me who loves horses and bikes and spiders and isn't freakin' *realistic.*"

Dad and Baba looked like they'd been struck by lightning. Mom adjusted the nose piece of her glasses.

Rosie tried to swallow the tomato chunk, but her throat closed. She briefly thought of spitting it out, but an image of Mom kneeling over the toilet and throwing up a meal flashed across her mind. *I am not like her.* She moved the tomato back into her cheek.

She rasped as if her vocal cords had been worked with a steel file. "You wish I'd never been born, because I'm not what you want. You're just like Michie's birth parents. You want to get rid of Divana's babies like they're nothing. You're probably planning to get rid of me and Jessie, too. It's so *easy* to throw people and animals away when they're not *perfect* like you!" Her nose dripped, darkening a pansy on the tablecloth.

"Are you serious, or are you being manipulative?" asked Mom coolly.

Rosie's sobbing escalated with being further misunderstood. It felt like her insides were going to come heaving out her mouth. Without thinking, she took a huge breath. The tomato she'd lodged in her cheek rode inwards with the air.

"She never cry like this before," said Baba.

Rosie gasped in staggered waves and clawed at her throat, then dropped to the floor. She wheezed, then stopped breathing. The skin along her jawbone turned blue.

Dad and Baba reached for her, but Mom was quicker. She fell on her knees, pushed Rosie on her side, wrapped her arms around her and squeezed. The blue veins on Mom's scant biceps bulged as she pressed against Rosie's padded ribs and middle.

Dad landed on all fours with a thud.

Mom squeezed harder, sweat beading her forehead. Rosie was still not breathing, and now her cheeks were blue.

Half-sitting, Dad placed his arms over Mom's. His big callused hands pressed on hers, which sank into Rosie's soft belly and pushed. After an eternal moment, Rosie again began to heave. The piece of tomato that had gone down her windpipe dropped from her mouth, accompanied by thick streams of saliva.

Rosie was now breathing hard. But breathing. She resumed sobbing.

"Oh my God, oh my God," said Mom over and over, stroking Rosie's sticky hair and massaging her back. "I'm so sorry, baby. You're my beauty, you're my beauty."

She lay down facing Rosie and pulled her hard, body to body, and cried with her. Her glasses flew off and skidded across the floor. The wire nose piece bent. "You *are* perfect for us. You've always been what I wanted. I'm the one who's not perfect. I keep trying and failing, worse each time. I'm mad at myself, Rosie, not you. At *myself*."

Dad lay right down on his side and wrapped his arms tightly around Mom and Rosie from behind. He wiped the spit and tears from Rosie's swollen face with the open collar of Mom's blouse. "You're my beauties," he said. "You've always been just perfect."

Baba planted her feet and put her hands, palms up, in the lap of her long skirt. Through a haze, Rosie heard her use the same guttural whisper as when she blessed Divana. She called on the Great Spider to weave the family together. They were suddenly all drenched with the golden medicine Rosie was just beginning to understand.

***

Rosie sat up gingerly. "Ouch," she said, and touched the thick bandage supporting her cracked rib.

Baba and Michie were sitting by her bed. "Love hurts," said Rosie with a grin.

"Only for little while," Baba replied. "It hurt to tell you it healing."

***

Michie responded enthusiastically to Rosie's plan to find homes for rescued animals. They scribbled ideas furiously on sheets of paper.

"Is excellent plan," said Baba. "I feel my heart heal while you talking. I love animal that never been hurt, like Billie. But there something extra special with one that was abused, then learn again to trust. They somehow deeper, inside."

Michie glanced away, her face flushed.

Rosie and Michie talked into the night. They surfed the 'Net, circled names in the Yellow Pages and used up two paper pads. Michie blew her most impressive bubble ever, twelve yellow inches across and gloriously delicate. Stronger threads of gum crisscrossed the surface. It didn't burst even when she and Rosie added an elbow bump to their secret handshake.

The next day, Rosie began making phone calls. Mr. Prockert from the rescue farm said, "Of course we'll participate. And I know just the people to contact."

CHAPTER SIXTEEN

The September Saturday dawned fine and soft. Rosie sat by her open window, through which the barest scent of autumn trickled in. She was watching Divana spin a new thread for her web. Michie scooped the last two dozen spiderlings into an aquarium and put the lid in place. Rosie had already put in the first three hundred and thirty two, with Baba counting, and said her farewells to the babies, imagining each one weaving their own and their families' futures. Michie's guy was already safe at her home.

"This is it, spider," said Rosie to Divana. "You and me, we've come a long way since you were a little frozen ball on the back steps. Thank you for everything. You're staying with me, but your babies have work to do in the world."

As Rosie and Michie carried the aquarium sideways out of the bedroom, Divana waved a front leg. At least two hundred spiderlings waved back. "I can't believe that just happened," said Michie.

"You haven't seen anything yet," Rosie replied. "Welcome to animal rescue world."

They placed the aquarium carefully on a pine table by the back steps.

On the porch, Aleisha, Peggy and Stefan rubbed their eyes and yawned one after the other. The group walked to the barn as a unit. Aleisha scooped oats for the horses. Peggy and Stefan broke open a bale of fragrant timothy hay. Once the horses were outside, Michie maneuvered the wheelbarrow so the others could shovel their stalls. Baba supervised wearing her brand new red cardigan.

The group trekked into the house, where they found Mom and Dad laying a breakfast feast on the table.

No sooner had they sat down, then vans, trucks and cars began arriving. From well down the road, the sound of alpacas beeping, dogs barking and horses whinnying could be heard. The air was fine crystal tinted pink, and the animals' voices rang in its stillness.

"They're here! They're here! And they're early!" said Rosie as she and her friends wolfed oatmeal and grabbed at buttered toast.

Leeanne and Christopher came to the door. "No thanks, we've eaten," said Chris to Dad's offer. "What can we do outside? Our parents are setting up the tables."

"The parking section signs went up last night, and everyone was mailed maps. But you could direct traffic and make *sure* no one puts dogs next to rabbits," said Rosie through a mouthful of apple juice. "We don't want any disasters."

Brad and Mark showed up next. They carried in several cardboard boxes with Cantonese writing on the side, and crammed down a few mouthfuls of Baba's apple *nalysnyky*, Ukrainian pancakes, before the entire group rushed out the door to help organize.

Rosie raced around surveying the landscape. The pasture, paddock and yard were dotted with open-sided white tents. Clouds of dust surrounded vehicles pulling cautiously into various parts of the farm.

Draft horses, tall lean horses and short, stout horses in a wide variety of colours, from the palest cremello to midnight black, together with a few ponies, a donkey and a Mammoth mule spilled from trailers in the middle of the three acre pasture. From a distance, they all looked healthy, glossy and well groomed. On closer inspection, the array of scars, bumps, and the frantic way some of them tore into their morning oats betrayed their past.

The horses called to each other with low nickers and shrill, beseeching whinnies. Jessie, Billie and Misha answered from inside the barn. Their humans double checked the knots on the ropes that tethered them to vans and fence posts. Rosie had a quiet word with Mr. Prockert, pointing out the location of the water tap and hose.

In the next enclosure were llamas, alpacas and goats, who gazed walleyed at the horses. Some were thin and missing patches of hair. Two "miniature" potbellied pigs, no longer small and therefore abandoned, eyed the mayhem suspiciously from their sturdy portable pen.

On the other side of the pigs was a table with several bird cages. Two budgies, blue and clear green, ruffled their feathers and chirped in the light that slanted into their tent, while a sulfur-crested cockatoo craned his neck and assessed the pigs with, "You're a pretty boy! You're a pretty boy!"

The pigs' snouts lifted proudly.

Peggy guffawed at the birds' antics and said, "Maybe my family will adopt one of these guys instead of bantam chickens. They really need homes."

"Great idea," said Rosie.

The man responsible for the birds leaned in and looked closely at her and Peggy. He pointed at the cockatoo and asked Peggy hopefully, "This one?" Rosie noticed he was wearing ear plugs.

The dogs were penned and tethered on the side of the barn in a paddock with a sturdy wire fence. Tiny hairy terriers yapped at a sprawling harlequin Great Dane. He pinned one down with a paw the size of its head and gently licked swirls into its back. A mountainous Rottweiler patiently allowed a mixed breed spaniel to bounce on her. The mutt growled and flung around a well-chewed bone, his ears like propellers.

Inside the barn, Jessie and Billie hung their heads over their stall doors, chewing hay and flicking their ears at the array of caged cats on tables. Some of the cats lounged in or on their sheltering boxes, while others glared at the horses. A three-legged tabby tom hissed at Billie, who dipped his nose into his water and flung it towards the cat, missing by bare inches. The feline looked outraged, but his hissing subsided.

"I see you have it all under control," said Rosie. Jessie raised her upper lip, exposing moist pink gums, and wagged her head. Rosie put her arms around the mare's glossy neck and gave her a warm hug. Jessie was shiny from her bath first thing that morning. "Take it easy, kitties," said Rosie. "It won't be long before you have homes. Jess, I'll be back in a tad to get you ready."

Baba and Misha were behind the barn. Baba had rolled her long skirt up in the waist so that the bottom edge of her green bloomers was showing. She was scrubbing Misha with one of Rosie's grooming cloths, now sopping wet. Both were covered in suds. "Baba, why is the water blue?" Rosie asked, alarmed.

"Bluing stuff make laundry sparkle white, it do same thing on horse. I use this on dorahenka goat Sonya in winter, when she depressed not having suntan. It work great."

Sunny maaaaaa-ed from his nearby pen. An *Already Adopted, Thank You!* sign strung to the wire moved in the light breeze. "Not you, banyak," Baba called. "You lucky, have some kind permanent tan."

"Ooo-kay," said Rosie. "Have you had a chance to look at the rescue animals?"

"Yes. Little bit. They all scared refugee, hoping for good home. You doing very good thing, Rosie."

The tall, handsome RCMP officer grooming his horse next to them nodded. Baba had met him at her singles club. "Because she always gets her man," Rosie told her friends.

Rosie put her hand lightly on Baba's back and said, "See you in the parade."

Near the house, in their own quiet section, were the rabbits. Angoras like huge puffballs, charming Flemish Giants and tiny Lop Ear bunnies shared their tables with a variety of guinea pigs.

Aleisha spoke eagerly with the volunteers as she cradled a huge white Californian rabbit. "Rosie," she said as her friend breezed by, "I think a bunny might be the perfect house pet for me and my grandma. She's not like the dog we had to leave in New Orleans, but maybe.." Her voice shrunk to a whisper. She tenderly stroked the head of the rabbit wearing a harness and leash. The rabbit purred loudly and pushed her black nose into Aleisha's armpit.

Rosie felt the golden medicine inside her glow, its rays reaching out to caress each creature and person who loved them. She sprinkled a little extra gold dust on Aleisha.

The bantam chickens were safely locked away in the tool shed, a *Do Not Open* sign nailed to the door.

Stefan had hosed out the wheelbarrow, and was delivering bales of hay to each section.

Brad, Mark and Michie were just finishing the set up on the table by the back door. Besides the spiderling aquarium, it held pyramids of white take out boxes and a wooden container with a top slot. Michie squared stacks of CDs, then anchored a stack of neatly typed pages with a fist-sized rock. A large hand-lettered sign said *Meet Divana's Darlings. Join our club.*

By ten a.m., the roads surrounding the farm were lined with cars. Rosie and her family had organized the event for the same weekend as the nearby agricultural fair, sent out media releases and bought a small ad in the program:

SECOND CHANCE PET ADOPTION FAIR

Open your heart to a rescued animal. A second chance can make a best friend.

Get a free lucky baby spider (if you want one).

Good homes only.

Foster parents welcome.

Rosie had persuaded local businesses to pay for a few hundred flyers. She and her friends spent hours on foot, bike and horseback delivering them to community bulletin boards and mailboxes. Baba had delivered stacks to her hair salon, singles club, bingo hall, and the Ukrainian Centre.

Dozens of people, including newspaper reporters, milled around the animals. Rescue workers cheerfully handed out pamphlets and interviewed prospective adopters. Within two hours, they had taken in adoption and foster home applications for half the animals. There were still four hours to go.

Rosie and Michie handed out typed sheets of paper with the Spider Song, to which Rosie had added a paragraph about how spiders brought her family luck, explaining a little of Baba and Dad's Ukrainian history and the return of Misha.

They gave out box after take out box of spiderlings to people who wanted them for their house plants, gardens and barns. In return, the spider adopters stuffed animal rescue donations into the wooden container. But before they were allowed to carry the babies away, Rosie asked them to raise their right hand.

"Repeat after me," she said. "I solemnly swear I will never kill a spider."

"I solemnly swear I will never kill a spider."

"I understand killing a spider will bring bad luck to me and my family for generations to come."

"I understand this will bring bad luck to me and my family for generations to come."

"If I am kind to spiders and other animals, they will bring good luck."

"If I am kind to spiders and other animals, they will bring good luck."

Two teenagers said, "What*ever*," and Rosie snatched the boxes from their hands.

A newspaper journalist snapped pictures of the ceremony. "Great job with the publicity, kid," she said.

"Thank you," Rosie replied. "I want the spiderlings to

spread all over BC. They'll bring good luck to thousands of people," said Rosie. "Best of all, they'll help abused animals find homes."

"Your idea and good work will spread farther than that," replied the journalist. "This event is going out to national press agencies and TV stations. This is a great thing you're doing here. I hope children in other cities organize rescues, too. Have you thought of starting a country-wide campaign?"

"Welllll," Rosie replied, "I have to finish grade eight first. But kids can e-mail me and ask for advice in the meantime."

"I'll let them know that."

The journalist smiled as she carried away her own box of spiderlings, complete with adoption certificate. The piece of paper certified her as a member of the *Divana's Darlings Club*. It held her to the promise, as all the adoption agreements did, that if she ever could not keep her pet, she had to contact the rescue organization first, for help. None of the pets could simply be sold or given away without Rosie and her family knowing where they were going.

Mom's face was soft and open. Her new eyeglass frames were a peach shade that added a blush to her cheeks. "I was so wrong," she said. "This is working out beautifully. It's like a miracle." She took care of selling CDs with Rosie singing the Spider Song, both the ancient version and her original lyrics. The proceeds were also going to animal rescue.

Dad and several neighbours guided parade participants to their places.

The parade started with the dogs, some wearing jackets with the name of their organization printed on the sides. They were led by volunteers and trainers who had chosen the best behaved. The Great Dane strutted under a fitted black horse blanket emblazoned with, *Let me be your puppy love*. Stefan led a fawn coloured mutt whose body was eight times the length of her legs. Aleisha carried a spotted chihuahua with a missing ear.

The llamas, alpacas and goats strode imperiously behind, sometimes tugged along by their handlers. Any dog that dared to stare back at them and even threaten a bark or lunge, received such a look down the patrician noses that he or she quickly turned away. Peggy mimicked the haughty expression on her own alpaca's face. A hairy black potbellied pig trotted earnestly behind, a blue bow in his tail.

The rabbits and birds sat out, as they'd be too stressed by parading.

Last came the horses. Colourful ribbons and yarn braided into their manes and tails flashed in the morning sun. The ones that were lame but had good personalities to be pasture pets, were led along. Brad and Mark proudly accompanied a pair of docile retired race horses. Their blankets said, *We're ReRuns.* Then it was time for the ones ready for new lives as riding horses. Leeanne and Christopher expertly displayed two of these, cueing them to prance and side pass.

Rosie, Michie, Baba and her new boyfriend were at the very end. Rosie was dressed in an immaculate white cotton shirt and breeches that contrasted starkly with her black leather boots and Jessie's coat. As they left the staging area, Rosie knotted the reins and balanced on the mare's bare back on her knees and hands. Michie flanked her on Smudge, a sedate bay gelding who had given years of lessons to children, then been abandoned in a field to starve.

Baba wore red satin pants and an embroidered blouse with puffy sleeves. Misha's coat was brightened to mirror lustre. They looked pristine except for the blue speckles on Baba's cheek and arm from Misha swishing her tail in the bluing water. Rosie didn't mention it.

As the three approached the crowd along the road, Rosie could see Mom and Dad leaning anxiously forward in the front row. She pushed off with her hands. Up, up, and she was half standing. She felt a hot twinge in the muscle covering her freshly knitted rib. She ignored it and shifted from foot to foot to balance. "Come on, Baba," she said, expecting her to do the trick they'd practiced together.

"No, Rosie," Baba replied, nudging Misha to keep up with Jessie's extended walk. "This your moment to make history, not mine."

Rosie saw the cameras ahead, and she wobbled, touching down lightly on her hands again. "Michie!"she whispered urgently. "Try this with me."

"No, Rosie," said Michie. "I'm not ready. But you are."

I am.

Rosie straightened all the way on Jessie's back, tall and proud, her arms spread against the sky. The black mare arched her neck and lifted her knees so that the sharp polished hooves knifed open the very air in front of her. Rosie leaned back and back from the waist until her outstretched arms were lifted by the wind, and she was soaring. She raised her chest until it would go no further.

Her ribs spread so far apart they began to separate from the rest of her skeleton. One after another, the bones sprang out in a spiral pattern. They formed a web of solid ivory strands that reached out to the four compass points of the earth, then the eight of the universe. Golden light radiated outwards from their ends.

Rosie's bones touched the planets, the galaxies, and the unknown future. She took one final breath of surrender. The skin, muscle and bone dissolved in the heat of the sun, and the highest point of her body was her open heart.

-The End-

Baba's Ukrainian Borshch

Hello kid, Baba here. I show you how to make special kind borshch, just like in Ukraina. You pay attention and do exactly what I say, or borshch not so good. Rosie, she learn how to make already when she just little tiny girl.

First thing, you ask grownup to help you. You need them to buy grocery things, and be watching while you fry and boil ingredient. Very important. Also, give self lots of time, because borshch must cook for many hour. This not modern original soup from can. Is real thing. Do not use crazy microwave for borshch. This make enough soup for four people for few day. For good party, make two, three time as much.

Now, go to store and buy:

Two pound oxtail. Other beef okay if not oxtail, but just okay. Nothing so good like oxtail for rich borshch. If your family vegetarian, ask grown up to show you make nice vegetable stock with lots garlic.

Three pound beet. If you can buy organic vegetable, so much better for you, the earth and also good tasting. Organic grow in horse manure, and nothing that come from horse can be bad.

One head green cabbage. No fancy-shmancy red or curly cabbage. Should be size your head. Little bit worm hole on outside leaf okay, let you know not much chemical on plant. Peel away this leaf. Ignore dirty look from store worker.

Two pound healthy carrot. If have dirt on them when you buy, so much better. Grown up probably make you wash them.

Two large onion. Do not buy kind already sprouting green at top. She busy having baby, not have time for you.

One head garlic. Start with usual size, maybe later you

like size elephant kind.

One large bunch fresh dill weed. Do not use kind dried up, come in salt shaker. That taste like straw. Pah! I spit on it.

One cup little white bean. These add protein, so borshch can be whole meal. Also turn pink when cooking with beets. Very cute. Later, when you get used to eating borshch, you might add more bean.

Whole black pepper. Enough so when you cup hand, just fit in your palm.

Little bit cheesecloth, needle and thread to sew whole black pepper in, drop into borshch. You also can use piece thin cotton sock. Make sure is clean, not smell like feet.

Four bay leaf. Be careful, have sharp edge.

Two pinch salt. Sea salt best. Tiny pinch, like you give brother, then pretend you not know why he mad.

Sunflower seed oil. From *soniashnyk,* kind we use in Ukraine.

Juice from three fresh lemons. Not frozen, not bottled. Fresh.

Two loaf dark rye bread. The kind so heavy you can use like football. Not modern Canadian white cotton bread.

One pound butter. If you can buy from farm, is better.

Tools: very large soup pot, large fry pan, chopping knife, slicing knife, soup stirring spoon and ladle, stirring spoon for fry pan, butter knife. Extra wooden spoon for smack hand of grown up person try to eat borshch before ready. Do not smack little brother or sister. Baba watching.

Okay kid, we get started now. You and grown up put on apron. **Put water in soup pot** about three quarter to top. Make boil. Make plan stay home that day. You have something to do, I know.

Drop garlic head and oxtail direct in borshch . Do not peel garlic. Let boil for at least four hour, maybe six, until some meat fall off bony part and floating in water. Add boiling water when necessary, so not run dry. That *boiling* water, not from tap. Make big difference to flavour. Then take bone out of water. Let bone cool on counter, because meat left make nice snack.

Grate beet, carrot and cabbage into big pile. Make sure peel beet. I don't peel carrot, it kill vitamin.

This part I can't tell you, **you have to use own brain**. Look back and forth from soup stock to vegetables. **Liquid should be about three-quarter of pot**. You want nice thick borshch, so look if you think vegetable fit in that liquid. Not too much, not too little. Should always be about one inch liquid on top vegetable. If too much liquid, either chop more vegetable or boil liquid more until some evaporate.

Chop fresh dill weed very tiny. Throw out stem.

Peel and chop onion. Put into big fry pan with sunflower seed oil. I not measure oil, nobody so stupid they can't see how much. Fry until onion soft and clear.

Put all vegetable carefully in soup pot. Be careful so they not splash hot water on you. Get grown up help.

Drop in little sewn up bag of whole black pepper. Do not be smarty pants, put pepper in without making bag. You be chewing terrible taste later.

Drop in four bay leaf. You can also make little bag for them, or just put in loose.

Pour in one cup white bean.

Add two pinch salt.

Now **have cool meat for nice snack** with grown up while wait for borshch to cook. See instruction below for how to eat with bread.

Make borshch cook two hour. Try by having grown up scoop white beans from bottom of pot, taste if they soft. Soup should be thick, almost like vegetable stew. Add more boiling water if too thick. In meantime, **squeeze lemon** and pour into glass jar. Put butter out so soft.

Scoop out black pepper and bay leaf. Throw away. Do not be lazy and leave in or borshch taste funny later. You can **keep soft garlic** to spread on top of buttered bread, if you like.

How to eat borshch: You think you know how eat

soup? Ha! Maybe terrible scary thing from can. Tuck napkin into shirt, because once redness of beet hit it, it not wash out. That why beet make good pysanka dye. Ladle nice thick borshch into bowl. Make sure you get bean from bottom, even you think you not love bean. You will now, Baba telling you this. Take thick slice butter onto dark rye bread. Not this skinny-shminny "spread" butter like is dangerous monster going to bite you. Add one teaspoon to one tablespoon lemon juice to soup. Take spoonful soup, blow on it. Eat soup, take bite bread. Or can dip buttered bread into soup. Try spread little soft garlic on top of butter. Keep eating.

Borshch taste even better, left in fridge overnight. Eat hot or cold.

If you like this recipe, tell grown up to buy Baba book, call *Baba's Kitchen: Ukrainian Soul Food*.

Book have all kinds of story about life in Ukraina, animals, and 190 good recipe.

www.ukrainiansoulfood.ca

There's more about Rosie's Rescue here:

www.reisastone.com

About the Author

Raisa Stone is a lifelong animal rescuer and horsewoman whose family first tamed horses over 5000 years ago in Ukraine.

She has travelled across the country as a professional horse groom and trainer, including at Spruce Meadows. She has her British Horse Society Pony Club Level 8, and has also shown dogs in conformation and obedience. She trains cats to walk on a leash, and also works to preserve land where wildlife can roam safe and free.

Besides writing, Raisa makes her living as an Animal Communicator and singer.

Learn about Animal Communication here:

www.reisastone.com

Made in the USA
Middletown, DE
16 December 2017